WOLF PACK

HIGHLAND WOLVES OF OLD, BOOK 1

TERRY SPEAR

PUBLISHED BY:

Wilde Ink Publishing

Wolf Pack

Copyright © 2022 by Terry Spear

Cover Copyright by Rainy Day Artwork

Discover more about Terry Spear at:

http://www.terryspear.com/

Print ISBN: 978-1-63311-085-4

Ebook ISBN: 978-1-63311-084-7

Tee Worrall, thanks so much for loving my books. I always love hearing from you and wish you all the best! Enjoy the trip to the past with the Medieval wolves of old!

SYNOPSIS

As wolves, Isobel, her kin, and a Highland slave are on the run from her Icelandic clan and now they must find a way to live in peace in Scotia without anyone discovering they are wolves or Vikings. Wearing traditional Icelandic clothes, sailing a Viking longboat, and speaking Gaelic with a Nordic accent, it won't be easy.

Alasdair is the wolf pack leader of his Highland clan, in the middle of adding fortifications to his castle when he spies what he thinks is a small Viking longboat—which can mean raiders and a fight. But what he discovers is two adult wolf females, a nearly grown male, and a female and male bairn on their shores. He can't imagine the family making the treacherous journey to his land all on their own, but he's captivated by Isobel, the woman who led her people to what she hopes will be safety.

Not everyone in his pack welcomes having Vikings living among them though. And Isobel is a wild and unpredictable woman, which fascinates him all the more.

1

After five weeks of sailing on the open ocean to Scotia, Isobel and her two nephews and a niece from the northlands, and a Scots slave, all gray wolf shifters, had finally arrived. But the coastline was rocky and dangerous, drifting fog hiding the peril that awaited them. She knew from the tales traders had shared with her Icelandic clan of the dangers that the fierce Scots posed to them as soon as they encountered them.

They hadn't had any choice. Once her uncle had failed to take over the clan to become the new chieftain and had lost his life, she and her nephews and niece were considered traitors as well, though they hadn't taken up arms against him. She'd freed Elene, the Scotswoman, who had taught Isobel and her kin the Scots' language, because she was a wolf like them and felt a kinship despite having different roots. When her parents' wolf pack had suffered large losses in their own clan, they had joined up with this chieftain until they could add to their wolf numbers again. It seemed it wasn't meant to be.

Isobel's extended family had been the only wolf shifters in

the clan, so she didn't feel any great loss in leaving the clan behind.

Elene was the same age as Isobel, just as passionate a fighter, just as eager to escape the tyranny of the chieftain and his people. But for Elene it was different. She would be returning to her homeland. Isobel and her kin were the enemy here. She was thankful Elene had told them to change their names to take on Scot's names to help hide their origin. Five weeks on the ocean had helped them to get more used to their new names.

Elene was just as worried about her reception in Scotia. She had been taken prisoner ten summers ago. Her parents had been murdered during the raid. Elene didn't even know if any of her own kin were still alive up north of here. Certainly, Isobel and her kin wouldn't be welcomed by Elene's people, no matter that they had freed her and brought her to safety. And no matter that they hadn't been a part of the clan that had killed off Elene's people and taken Elene hostage either. They still had Viking heritage.

Landing the longboat safely on the beach beyond the breakers was now Isobel's current dilemma.

Conall was shouting orders to his younger siblings. He would be ten and five years in two more months. His mother and father had named him Bodolf—wolf leader. Someday, he might be. But not this day. He had balked at changing his name until Elene told him Conall meant strong wolf in Gaelic, so he was fine with that.

He was a good navigator, but Isobel was still in charge. She was ten and nine and she'd navigated these waters since she'd been eight. Both her mother and father had been eager to teach her how to lead a party to the Scots' land once her twin brother had been lost at sea. She'd never thought she would be leading her kin on a journey like this while escaping their clan and she had never considered she would be bringing them to Scotia to live. The only way she would have ever gone there was to trade with the Scots, or fight battles, which it often led to.

Their mother had died in an earlier battle between Norse clans, like Isobel's own mother and father had. To protect her niece and nephews and herself from ill treatment—or worse, Isobel had hurried them to pack food, water, tools, weapons, and furs, anything they could use to survive on the journey and for when they arrived in Scotia. Then they'd sneaked Elene out of the longhouse where she was staying and had stolen away before the chieftain could decide their fate. They had taken the long, perilous journey in a small longboat her uncle had owned before the chieftain seized it. Isobel had hoped when they made it to Scotia, it would be a new way of life and freedom for them. But what if they became slaves of the Scots? She couldn't think of that.

"We will break up on the rocks before we reach the shore," Conall warned.

"We willna." Isobel cast him a scolding look. She had to keep the younger ones' spirits up. Libby was spirited, but right now, the girl of five summers looked haunted. She was half hidden under her long wool shawl. Drummond was seven summers and had been born at sea during one of their mother and father's expeditions. A water giant—his mother had named him—or a sea monster—because he'd been such a big baby and hard to deliver. He loved the sea most of all.

All of them were drenched in sea water, the sun having dried them off, leaving them caked in salt. They'd survived on fresh fish they'd caught, smoked fish they'd brought with them, flat bread, and fresh water.

Elene was quiet as usual, as if she were still a slave in the clan's village.

"You can speak your mind now," Isobel said. "You are our friend, not a slave any longer."

Elene nodded, her hair as matted as all of theirs was, braided with beads, just like theirs was, though her hair was dark while their hair was the color of spun gold.

Their cheeks and the tips of their noses wore a red glow from the constant sun, though they'd encountered severe storms also during their journey. The waterproof tent in the middle of the longboat had protected them and their supplies to a degree and they'd taken turns sleeping beneath it. A brazier had provided heat and they used it to cook any fish they had caught.

Isobel was glad to finally see the shore so close by. But the fog kept drifting in sheets across the shoreline, revealing it briefly and hiding it again. She was afraid they'd break up their longboat before they could reach the shore. Oceanwater was striking the rocks and breaking up, splashing sky high, warning them of the danger of the partially submerged rocks.

"We need to navigate over there," Isobel said, pointing to what appeared to be a narrow passage where the water was deeper and she didn't detect any breaking water, and they might just make it to shore. Then they'd have to hide their Viking longboat just in case they needed to escape to somewhere else. Not to mention they didn't want it exposed to the cliffs where someone could see it from up above and know they had landed and then the search would be on for them.

"There's a cave over there," Elene said, pointing to treacherous currents flowing into the cave.

"Let's make our way there." Isobel steered them in that direction.

With the sail down, they rowed toward the narrow passage between the rocks, scraping the sides of the longboat. Everyone's hearts were beating frantically, and Isobel's young niece gasped when they hit a rock. They finally managed to maneuver until they could angle into the mouth of the cave.

When they managed to enter the cave without breaking the

longboat up on the rocks, it was dark inside, except for the light shining into the mouth of the large cave. But just as quickly, fog rolled in, swallowing them up, as if to blanket them in secrecy, protecting them from the Scots who might wish them dead.

Isobel took that as a good sign. The gods were with them—this time anyway.

~

ALASDAIR SWORE he had seen something in the water—a small longboat—a Viking longboat. He'd seen the red-and-white striped sail first, and then it was gone. Then he saw the longboat and then it disappeared, saw it again, and it vanished yet again behind large swells of waves. But when he reached the edge of the top of the cliffs, he saw naught but the waves crashing onto the rocks a way out from shore and fog quickly enveloping the whole area.

His brother Hans quickly joined him and slapped him on the back. "I told you there was naught out there. Did you see a serpent again?"

Alasdair was certain he'd seen a hand-carved figurehead of a dragon at the prow of a small longboat leading the way. The dragon was meant to placate the gods of the sea and ensure its safe voyage. A *Viking* dragon.

They hadn't had any trouble with the Norsemen here of late because of how treacherous the waters were. But it didn't mean they wouldn't have difficulties with them at some later date. He had traded with some but fought with others. He never knew when to trust them. Language was a barrier. And their intent—peaceful or not—could be an issue also.

For a while, Alasdair stared down at the beach, but he couldn't see anything. Nor could he make out any sounds other than the water crashing into the rocks. With his enhanced wolf hearing, he suspected he would catch the sound of the breaking up of a vessel on the rocks, or men talking, injured or otherwise, as they made it to shore.

"Dinna worry. If Vikings managed to land on the shore—which they have not, or we would see them—they will never make it up the steep cliffs."

The Norsemen were persistent, if nothing else. If they had arrived and not broken up on the rocks, they would find a way to climb up the cliffs, he was certain.

But what he couldn't understand was that the sailing vessel had been smaller than what he was used to seeing Viking raiders used. Like a fishing vessel, not a ship sailing on the open seas. Unless they'd had an armada and this one was the only one left or had lost the rest of the longboats in a storm and the rest of the armada was far from here. The other thing that puzzled him was that the figures on the vessel had seemed a wee bit small—not like hulking Viking raiders and that didn't make any sense either.

"Do you want to post a guard to alert us if raiders actually do make it to our shores?" Hans asked, when Alasdair didn't budge from his spot.

Alasdair wanted to be the one keeping watch. "Is the boar done cooking?"

"Aye, that's why I came to fetch you. But if you want me to stay—"

The sky was darkening, the twinkling of green lights of female fireflies telling prospective males they were ready to mate filled the night.

"Nay, let's eat. You're right. I just imagined seeing a serpent in the sea. 'Tis naught but my imagination playing tricks with me." Which happened from time to time as unpredictable as the weather was along the coastline.

2

Alasdair was the pack leader of thirty wolves—his brothers, Hans and Rory, and their sister Bessetta— and the other wolves he'd taken into the pack who had needed guidance and were agreeable to his rule. Not that they didn't have squabbles among them, but since there were fewer of the wolf shifters than humans, they did tend to stick together.

"While we were cooking the boar, what were you doing?" Bessetta asked, then took a bite of her cooked meat in the great hall.

"Alasdair was watching the ocean for the Viking raiders about to attack our village and the keep," Hans said, the story-teller of the bunch. "We should have worked faster on finishing the wall."

Everyone looked up from their meal to see what Alasdair had to say about it. Even though they could guess Hans was making up a story, the threat of Vikings on their land could be real.

Alasdair shrugged and took a bite of the boar. Alasdair and his siblings had been born to their mother at the same time—

well, a few blinks of an eye apart. He was the oldest, Bessetta, the youngest, and Hans was the next oldest, Rory in between him and Bessetta.

"Tell us what you think you saw," Rory said, "before Hans makes up more of a tale and we don't know what to think."

"I thought I saw a Viking ship sailing on the ocean headed for our shore. But you know how it is with the waves kicked up by the recent storms and the fog rolling in, covering everything in its path. I'm not sure what I saw, or if I saw anything at all."

All eyes were upon him still, as if they believed he had seen something, and the danger could be very real to all of them. But if he had thought so, he would have had someone serving on guard duty, watching the beach.

"But?" Rory asked.

Alasdair shook his head. "It looked like the size of a fishing longboat, but the prow had a dragon figurehead. And the sailors looked like wee bairns."

Everyone laughed. That certainly didn't inspire fear in them.

"That's why I dinna believe it was anything more than my imagination. If it was not just me imaging things, they would still have to navigate the rocks and climb the cliffs. Not an easy feat, either one."

"Yet you were able to envision that much," Bessetta reminded him, sounding like she believed he'd seen what he thought he'd witnessed.

"The fair folk," Rory said. "Naught more."

"Aye," Hans said. "Do you think we should post a lookout, just in case what you think you might have seen is true?"

Alasdair ate some more of the boar, then nodded. "Aye. You can schedule the men for the duty. I will take watch before dawn."

"I will take watch before gloaming," Bessetta said.

They all did their part in the clan—men and women alike

—though if they had to deal with Vikings, he didn't want his sweet sister to learn the hard way that what he'd seen was right.

He nodded. "As a wolf."

"Aye." Though Bessetta could fight well with a sword and *sgian dubh*, he still wanted her to serve on duty as a wolf.

She could run faster, howl even, if she spied the enemy. Though as a human, they could howl also. If Vikings were making the dangerous climb up the cliff face, he would think of them as his foe.

"I can go with her," Rory said.

Alasdair ate another slice of boar. "Nay. We have work to do, sleep to catch up on, guarding of our village and castle. If Bessetta canna do this on her own, she will stay at the keep, and you will go instead."

"Nay," Bessetta said, giving Rory a reproachful look.

Rory smiled at her, loving to tease their younger sister.

"If they are below the cliffs and Bessetta or anyone else on guard duty hears them trying to climb up, if they are far below, dinna howl. Just return and report what you've seen. But if anyone doesna hear them until it is too late, howl and run like the wind. Dinna try and stop them. A well-placed arrow not only could kill you—" Alasdair said.

"But reveal the truth about us," Hans said. "Which is *much* worse."

It wasn't that they thought if one of their people died it didn't matter. It did. As a wolf pack, they were close to each other—family, kin, and more. One death greatly affected them all. But if any of them died as a wolf, they would turn into their human form. They couldn't let on they were wolf shifters to non-wolf shifters. When they battled it out with other clans, they only did so in their human form. Though if they were wholly outnumbered and could slip away into the woods, they could remove their clothes, hide them to return for them later, shift, and run as a wolf.

Alasdair noticed then that Bessetta had left the great hall and he looked around for her.

"If you are looking for Bessetta, she is off shifting in her chamber so she can run to the cliffs and see if you were right or no'," Hans said.

Alasdair let out his breath and leaned over closer to speak to him more privately as other conversations were shared over the meal about catching dragons in the water, seeing the fair folk, and other such things. "Go with her, just to make sure no one has breached the cliffs. If everything is quiet and you see no trouble, then you can leave her to her task and return until it's your turn to be a guard, Hans."

"Aye, will do."

Alasdair trusted his sister to do a good job watching for trouble but if the trouble had already breached the top of the cliff, he didn't want her to be running for her life.

Alasdair drank some more of his ale and then waved his tankard at Bessetta as she came to the table as a blond wolf, her belly and chin white, and woofed at him. "Go and be vigilant. Hans will go with you just to make sure no one has already climbed the cliffs unbeknownst to us." Not that he thought anyone would have, or that anyone was down below the cliffs, or he would have seen a longboat on the beach or heard it wrecked on the rocks, but just to be certain, he wouldn't risk his sister's life.

Then she licked Hans's hand and the two of them took off for the cliffs.

"You sent Hans with her but no' me," Rory said, sounding a bit miffed, as if Alasdair hadn't trusted his younger brother to keep her safe.

But Alasdair did. "Aye, but only to make sure everything's fine, not to stay with her."

Appearing to understand Alasdair's reasoning, Rory nodded. "I want to go as a man when I serve on guard duty."

Alasdair shook his head. "As a wolf." Then he said louder for everyone to hear, "Everyone will go as wolves who serve on guard duty. You can howl and warn us of trouble and outrun an arrow if you're quick enough. On your own against a bunch of Vikings if you're armed only with your sword and shield, you would no' be able to stand against them."

A chorus of "ayes" by the men and women in the great hall filled the air.

Alasdair hoped he was wrong about spying a longboat in the ocean—that he had only imagined it. He'd had the strangest dreams of late, though he hadn't shared them with his brethren, afraid they might see them as a bad omen.

He'd been fighting with a beautiful, golden-haired, Viking shieldmaiden. Swords clashed and she was damn good at it too. A worthy foe. He'd seen wolves that were not his own in attendance, ready to protect her and he was all alone. Maybe that's why he thought he'd seen a Viking longboat.

It was all just a manifestation of his dreams.

~

"I want to get out of the longboat," Isobel's young niece, Libby, said.

Isobel didn't blame her. She was ready to get out of the longboat too. Because of how long they'd been rocking in the boat, it would take some getting use to when they stood on stationary land again.

Elene said, "If anyone saw us from the top of the cliffs while we were coming into shore, they could be watching from up there. What are we going to do?"

"I'll climb up and see if it's safe for us to go up that way." Isobel was worried about getting her younger niece and nephew up the cliffs. She wasn't sure about Elene either. She knew Conall could manage.

"I should go," Conall said.

She shook her head. "I brought you here. If something happens to me, then you have to take care of your brother and sister and you will be making the decisions from then on."

Conall looked at Elene. "What are you going to do?"

Isobel hadn't asked the question of Elene, hoping she'd stay with them, but she could understand if she wanted to try and make her way home to see if she could find any of her family that might still be alive. And Isobel felt it was her obligation to make sure she got there safely. Even though Isobel and her family would be at risk for doing so, Elene wouldn't be safe traveling alone either. Not as a single woman.

"If you allow me too, I'll stay with you for the time being." Elene felt like part of Isobel's family because she was a wolf like them. And she'd taught them her language whenever they were beyond the clan's hearing.

"I'm glad you will." Isobel was sincere about it. She really liked the woman who was always quiet, though that might have been because she'd been a slave.

Now that Elene was home, Isobel wondered if she would act differently. So far, she hadn't. But if she found some of her family, would she then feel surer of herself? Isobel suspected it would be so.

Elene sighed. "You were the only ones who were kind to me when the others in your clan weren't."

"That's because we weren't really members of the clan," Conall said, sounding angry. "And you are a wolf like us. That makes us family, dinna you think?" He ran his hands through his tangled blond hair. "I should have helped our da when he fought the chieftain."

"We would have been dead," Isobel said. "He never told us his plans. And it all happened so quickly. Whoever was supposed to help him overthrow the chieftain didn't side with him like they had pledged." That had angered her. Not that they would have been successful if they hadn't turned on him, but she hated them for backing out on her uncle.

Conall lit a lantern and they looked at the cave more closely. It was getting dark, and they found the cave went back a long ways and they could use loose rocks to pile up on the towline so that when the tide went out, they wouldn't lose their longboat out to sea. Though it would probably smash up on the rocks first if it got loose from its mooring.

Conall got out of the longboat and secured it, and then Isobel handed up some of their furs and food and he carried them deeper into the cave. "Just be careful," he said. "It's slippery in here."

"And damp and chilly." But their furs would keep them warm. Isobel climbed out of the longboat and helped Libby out, and then Drummond. She grabbed Elene's hand and assisted her onto the cave floor. Then they made a bed out of the furs. "Before first morning's light, I'll start the climb." At least as wolves, they could see in the dark, so they had the advantage. She just had to go early enough so that she could make it to the top of the cliff without being seen. And then, if it was clear and there were no settlements nearby, she could howl to her kin and Elene, and they'd know it was safe to come up.

She figured for now, they'd leave their belongings in the cave and only take what they needed to eat and weapons also to protect themselves, of course.

"We need to wear the clothes of my people," Elene said.

Isobel and her kin had been speaking Gaelic the whole time they'd been on the ocean to improve their use of it, but they still had accents that set them apart from the Scots.

"*Ja*," Isobel said. "Aye."

"We could steal them, if we find a croft," Conall said.

Isobel hated to steal from people who probably couldn't afford to have many clothes. But they needed to disguise themselves the best they could. Elene was right. It could mean the difference between life and death.

"Are you sure you don't want me to climb the cliffs first?" Elene asked. "My Gaelic is much better than yours."

"It is, but, nay, you're still dressed like us."

"I...I canna say enough of how grateful I am to you that you freed me." Elene sighed. "I didna think I would ever get out of there, or even that I would meet you and your family and that we would have so much in common."

"Aye. I wanted in the worst way to free you from that first meeting. It killed me to see the way they treated you," Isobel said.

"The chieftain didn't like that all of you were kind to me. It would have been worse if you had left me behind."

"We would never have left you behind," Isobel said. Even though sneaking her out had put them more at risk, because she was a wolf like them, they'd had to free her no matter what.

Libby snuggled up next to Isobel and she wrapped her arms around her niece. For now, they were safe. But how long would that last? She was afraid they would soon find out they weren't safe at all.

~

EARLY THE NEXT morning before the sun rose, Isobel and the rest of her companions took turns stripping and shifting and doing their business near the cliffs as wolves. If anyone saw them, they wouldn't believe wolves could be on the shore when they wouldn't have any way to climb down the cliffs to get there in the first place. But they wouldn't suspect they were anything other than wolves or maybe even wild dogs. Not Vikings.

Then they returned to the cave and once Isobel had shifted and dressed, she said, "Conall, you're in charge of your sister and brother. Stay in the cave until I return and let you know it's safe. Elene, you're a free woman. I hope you stay with them, but it's your choice."

Elene smiled. "I'll stay with them."

It was a balancing act for Isobel. Conall was responsible for his siblings, and Isobel was responsible for all of them. She hoped Elene stayed with them because Isobel wanted to keep her safe also, but she understood if at some point Elene wanted to be on her own since she wasn't related to them by blood. Though what if all wolves at some point had been?

"I'll stay with them," Elene said again.

"Thank you." Isobel gave her a hug, and then hugged her younger nephew and niece.

Conall always acted like he was too old or too much of a warrior for hugs, but she pulled him into her arms and embraced him. "Keep them safe."

"I will."

Then she left the cave and hurried to the cliffs, praying she wouldn't be seen by anyone who might be up on top, though she couldn't imagine why anyone would be. As soon as she reached the cliffs, she looked for the best hand and footholds and began the climb, praying she didn't fall and leave her kin and Elene alone to fend for themselves in a hostile world.

3

Early that morning before first light, Alasdair was taking the last watch as a wolf at the cliffs. Others would come throughout the day, but if they didn't see anyone on the beach by midday, he figured it would mean he'd only thought he'd seen a longboat and there had been nothing to it.

When he drew close to the edge of the cliff, he heard a rock falling down the rockface close to the top. He couldn't imagine rocks falling for no reason. If they had been experiencing a landlash, strong winds, or punishing rain—mayhap. The other possibility? Someone was climbing to the top.

He peered over then and saw a golden-haired woman climbing up the rockface and his heart nearly gave out. She bewitched him, her hair partly loose, and some of it in braids. She fascinated him not only because of her blond locks, but for the garments she wore—deer hides fashioned into trewes and a tunic, and leather belts that showed off her slim figure and leather boots trimmed with fur. She was a Norsewoman, he was certain, and he wondered if her longboat had broken up on the rocks and she had swum to shore, dried out, and was now trying to reach the top of the cliffs so she could find food and shelter.

She appeared to be alone and wouldn't pose any threat to him or his pack members unless others of her kind came to rescue her. Though he could see she was armed with a sword, and probably a dagger hidden in her boot.

She suddenly looked up as if she realized someone was watching her. He ducked away from the edge. He didn't want to scare her if she should see a wolf watching her and she worried he would attack her. Though he wouldn't. He wanted to watch her progress, help her should she have trouble, but he couldn't as a wolf. And if he shifted, how would that look? A naked Scotsman coming to pull her up on top of the cliffs? She wouldn't understand.

He tore off into the nearby woods so when she crested the cliff he wouldn't be seen as a threat. He strained to listen for any sounds that said she was still climbing the cliff. He was dying to know if she was nearly to the top. He wasn't sure what he was going to do after she reached the top. He guessed he would follow her wherever she went and stay out of her line of sight. He wouldn't howl to alert the others. Not since there was only one of them.

She finally reached the top but didn't climb the rest of the way. She just peered around at the scenery, the mountains in the distance, the woods, the loch while he watched her and waited. He assumed she was afraid to reveal herself, but no one was about and still, she didn't climb on top of the cliffs. What was she waiting for?

Then to his surprise, she disappeared below the edge of the cliffs. No way could she be climbing back down to the beach below. What if she had been the scout? And there were others hiding down below and he hadn't seen them?

He ran toward the cliffs until he reached them and slowly

peered over the edge. He saw the top of her head as she continued to make her way down the cliffs. Others had to be hiding down below somewhere, though he couldn't imagine where. Unless...there were caves down there? None of his people had ever climbed down there. There hadn't been any reason to.

Still, he didn't howl, wanting to see just where she was going once she reached the bottom of the cliffs. He was amazed at how agile and strong she was. That was a long climb to make.

He was lying down, keeping a low profile, peering over the edge. She didn't look up while she was descending, too busy keeping her footing. Once she was down, he backed off, afraid she'd look up. Then he heard her running across the rocky shore and he moved to the edge again, staying low, peering down.

He expected to see a whole bunch of Viking men coming to greet her, though he wondered why they wouldn't send one of them to climb up the cliffs instead of one of their women. Though Alasdair knew their women fought as ferociously as the men.

She paused near the water's edge, and he anticipated she'd glance back at the cliff to make sure no one was watching her, which she did. He ducked out of sight, hoping she hadn't seen his head. She might have thought he was a villager's dog and would warn the villagers she was here.

He finally chanced looking over the cliff again, but she was gone.

~

"WELL?" Conall asked. "What did you see, Isobel?"

"Forests, a loch off in the distance. It's a strenuous climb and

I think that just you and I should go, if Elene is all right with it and she can stay with the younger ones," Isobel said.

Conall was all for it, but Elene was quiet.

"I want to go," Drummond said.

"Nay. You stay with your little sister. You'll both come with us once we scout around and learn what we can," Isobel said. She glanced at Elene. "What do you think?" She had to remember that Elene was from this land, and she would know the people and their customs better than Isobel and her kin would.

"I believe I should go with you, or with Conall, should you choose to stay with the wee ones. I'm a Scot and they'll know it. I can do all the speaking for us. But we could also run into danger. Like with your people, mine also have clan fights and so we won't know which clans are in this area and if they were friend or foe of my own people."

Conall looked ready to object, but then he said, "I'll stay behind. As much as I dinna want to, my brother and my sister are my responsibility, and two women may no' be seen as much of a threat. They would be wrong, but they wouldna know it."

"You saw no one up there?" Elene asked Isobel.

"No one. I heard the birds in the trees singing away, no voices, saw no movement other than birds flitting about the woods. We take our bows and see if we can bring back something to eat and we'll fill our waterskins at the loch. While we're gone, you three gather wood and take it into the cave. We'll try to start a fire behind the rocks there, that jut out from the cave's entrance. It would hide our fire from anyone on the water," Isobel said.

"What about from the cliffs?" Conall asked.

"They could see the smoke. If the wind is blowing in the right direction, we could have a fire near the entrance of the cave so that it willna smoke us out, but we can warm up, dry out, and cook a meal. Or we could use the brazier, if we didn't smoke

ourselves out. Just gather the driftwood and we'll decide after we
return. Are you ready, Elene?" Isobel asked.

"Aye, let's go."

Then the two women ran across the beach and to the cliffs as
fast as they could go. Elene was wearing trewes also, instead of a
kirtle that the women wore. They had taken Isobel's parents'
and her aunt and uncle's clothing to use for additional warmth
and to change into when they were too wet.

At one point, Isobel swore she saw a wolf peering over the
cliff at them, but it was gone so quickly, she had to have been
mistaken. The first time up the cliffs had been wearying, but the
second time, she was getting winded. Elene was doing well, and
Isobel was glad for that. They worked hard in the clan, so they
were in good shape, not to mention all the rowing that they had
done for weeks at sea whenever they were becalmed.

When they finally reached the top, Isobel peered over first,
and seeing the way was clear, she climbed up on top. Then she
helped Elene the rest of the way and the two raced across the
meadow grasses to the safety of the forest, but she was surprised
to smell a wolf had been there. A male wolf. Watching them. At
the cliff's edge.

"Did you smell a male wolf?" she asked Elene, whispering
the words.

"Aye. One of our kind? Or a real wolf though?"

"I dinna know." Wolves could be territorial, either kind.
Isobel was surprised. If their kind lived in the area—Scots' wolf
shifters, not Norse wolf shifters—would they be more receptive
to taking them in? Or would they want to eliminate them,
fearing they were here to fight them for their land? Or steal from
them?

As soon as they reached the woods, Isobel felt they were
being watched. She looked around but didn't see anyone. Her
skin prickled with unease.

"Do you sense it too?" Elene asked. "That we are being watched."

"Aye." That's when Isobel saw a wolf and then another. They were suddenly surrounded by wolves. They didn't dare ready their bows. There were too many of them. All Isobel thought about was poor Conall and her little niece and nephew and how they had led them into a trap.

One of the wolves suddenly shifted into a tall man—with glorious dark brown hair, a beard, dark brown eyes and the rest of him was well-muscled. He appeared to be a warrior and he was truly beautiful to look at. She should have been alarmed to see him naked before her, but she was—impressed. He was looking at Elene and Isobel chanced to look at his remarkable staff, but when her gaze returned to his face, she saw he was looking her straight in the eye, a small smile settling on his lips. She was definitely blushing.

"I am Alasdair, these are my pack members, and you are wolves trespassing on our land. Who are you and what do you want?"

Isobel's mouth gaped. He was the pack leader? She thought he would want to kill her right there, but he seemed—reasonable—at least at the moment.

"We mean no one any harm," Elene quickly said. "We were slaves of an Icelandic clan up north and escaped from there, traveling for weeks to get here."

"You are a Scot," Alasdair said, sounding surprised.

"Aye. The Norsemen killed my family. I dinna know if any of them survived," Elene said, with tears in her eyes.

It was the first time Isobel had seen Elene shed tears and she wanted to hug her and comfort her when the man called Alasdair said, "You are welcome to join us. Where is your longboat?"

Isobel bit her lip. She didn't want to tell them about their longboat or about her niece and nephews in case these men turned out to not have their best interests at heart.

"We were shipwrecked," Elene quickly said, and Isobel was glad she was such a quick thinker.

"Oh?" Alasdair sounded like he didn't believe her. "Is anyone else waiting below the cliffs for you?"

"Nay," Isobel said too ferociously and with her Icelandic accent. She shouldn't have said anything like Elene had told her not to.

"Just the two of us made it to shore," Elene said.

"Who else was with you? More slaves of the Icelanders that chanced to escape?" He sounded like he didn't believe her.

Isobel didn't think that sounded believable either, but she waited for Elene to say something further.

"You couldna have manned a longboat all that time, just the two of you, and they wouldn't have brought you to our lands, risking your escape." Alasdair took a deep breath and let it out, as if he was going to let them off at their word—at least for the time being. "Come, we will feed you and provide you shelter, and you can tell us more about your people." But he continued to eye Isobel with suspicion, and she knew she shouldn't have spoken a word.

She would have to, though, when they questioned them further. She couldn't pretend to be a mute.

Then Alasdair shifted into his wolf and motioned for the others to take the women with them.

At least Alasdair hadn't shifted and then disarmed them. That made her feel safer. Until a wolf howled from behind her, and more wolves howled beyond the forests and the loch. How many were there?

She glanced around her, thinking Alasdair was following behind them, making sure they didn't try to escape, which would have been foolish on her and Elene's part.

They had nowhere else to go and if they climbed back down the cliffs, these men would learn who else was down there, find the longboat and their supplies. Isobel and her companions would have lost all of it. She really thought Alasdair would lead the way. Then again, her father had told her that he followed behind their small wolf pack when they were traveling to ensure no one was left behind.

But Alasdair had disappeared into the woods.

~

ALASDAIR HOWLED for his men in the village to bring his clothes with them to the cliffs. He and a few of his men would descend the cliffs and learn just how many Vikings were down there while the others would take the two women back to their castle. He couldn't believe the women were wolves and he knew they hadn't come alone. Though if they were correct in saying they were the only two who had survived a shipwreck, that was possible but not likely. He was certain he would have seen some remnants from a shipwreck also. And neither woman looked like they'd been injured in the least. They were carrying several water pouches, and he suspected they had planned to fill them with water from the loch to return to the others down below.

They were also carrying bows, arrows, and *sgian dubhs* so he assumed they had planned to hunt for their meal.

The one woman was most likely a Scotswoman, dark-haired, dark eyed, very pretty. She was the one doing most of the talking until the other one was afraid he and his men would check the shore for other "survivors" of a shipwreck. It was possible the women were alone, but he had to make sure of it. The other woman, beautiful blue eyes and golden haired, was an Icelander. He was certain of it. Unless she'd been captured when she was very young, and her language had been influenced greatly by the Norsemen who had raised her.

As soon as his men rode to him on horses, bringing his own with them along with his clothes, he shifted, dressed in his tunic, brat, and boots, securing his belt, sword, and *sgian dubh*, and mounted the horse. Then they rode from the woods to the cliff's edge. When they reached it, he and the others dismounted. He peered over the edge and this time he saw a young man and two bairns gathering firewood. The youngest was wearing a brown kirtle and leather shoes, a shawl around her shoulders. A young lassie. The next oldest was a lad, not much older than the lass. He wore a gray tunic and trewes and was running barefoot in the sand on the warm summer's morn. The older lad was tall, but not well-muscled yet, his tunic a muted green while his breeches were tan in color, and he was ordering the young ones about.

"You missed a few sticks over there," he said to the younger lad.

Alasdair couldn't believe it. Could just the five of them manage to make it all that way from Iceland on their own? Grown men had to be with them.

Armed with swords, Alasdair and five of his men began the climb down the cliffs. They would use ropes to bring the bairns up. The younger ones wouldn't be able to make the ascent on their own.

The three of them saw the men climbing down the cliffs and dashed off beyond the cliffs, and Alasdair realized there had to be a cave there as the three of them disappeared like the woman had before.

Alasdair and his men finally made it down to the shore and he called out, "We mean you no harm. We will take you in, feed you, and provide you shelter and clothes."

They crossed the beach until they could reach the cave

entrance, and stood nearby, not showing themselves to whoever was in the cave, just in case they were attacked. Not by the three bairns, but by warriors who could be inside the cave just waiting for them.

At first, he thought maybe the women were the only two who were wolves, but he smelled the older lad and two bairns had left their scents on the beach and they were wolves also.

He'd never encountered Icelandic wolves before. But he still wondered if there were more inside, waiting to fight him. "Come on out. We have taken the women back to our keep to feed them," Alasdair said. "The bairns canna climb the cliffs on their own. The women willna return for you. We are providing them shelter at the castle. You must come with us."

The older lad finally came out then, brandishing a sword, a fierce expression on his determined face. He was going to protect the younger ones with all his might.

Alasdair smiled. "We are wolves like you. And if you are a well-trained warrior, but most of all a hunter and a farmer, we can use you in our pack."

The lad stared at him in surprise.

"I'm Alasdair, the leader of the pack. Our pack is thirty wolves strong. And you are?"

"Thirty?" The lad looked even more shocked.

"Aye."

The lad stood straighter. "I'm Bodolf."

Viking for wolf leader. They were Vikings.

"I mean..." Bodolf hesitated. "Conall."

Alasdair opened his mouth and nodded. Gaelic for wolf. He was a Viking. "And the others?"

"My sister, Libby, and brother, Drummond." Conall ducked back into the cave and had to usher them out, holding the girl's hand, her eyes wide. Conall was still holding his sword so he couldn't hold the boy's hand too, but he looked like he wished Conall would.

Then Alasdair and some of his men had to take a look in the cave to ensure no warriors were hiding in there, but other than finding a seaworthy longboat with a dragon leading the way—which surprised him given how dangerous it was to navigate the narrow passage between the breakers and into the cave—furs, clothes, tools, a brazier, weapons, and food, that's all they discovered in the cave.

Alasdair couldn't believe they had made it all the way here in the small longboat—just the five of them, and two so young, he assumed they would not have been very much help. "We'll leave the longboat here, in the event you need it at some point, but we'll bring your supplies with us so you can use them while you stay with us." Alasdair wanted them to know they were free to stay with the pack or leave as they wished. They didn't take slaves or force wolves to join them.

"This is my brother Hans and when I'm not in charge, he is. And Rory, who is with the women, is my other brother. We also have a sister, Bessetta, and she'll help look after your needs. Let's get you up the cliffs." Alasdair had the men carry their supplies to the cliffs and while they hauled them up, they made a harness for the younger lad first.

Conall stayed with his sister while his brother was hauled up, looking like he was unsure what to do. Conall didn't appear to want to leave his sister alone with the strangers, nor did he want his brother taken away from him either. Alasdair completely understood how he was feeling.

"We can take your sister up now and you can climb on your own, aye?" Alasdair asked.

"*Ja.* Aye."

They had learned to speak Scots well and Alasdair wondered if it was because the one Scotswoman had been a

slave and taught them their language. That would make it easier
for all of them to understand each other in the pack and as long
as they didn't cause trouble among his clan, he welcomed them
as family.

After they finally had the bairns up on top of the cliff, along
with their older brother, each of them rode with one of his men
and they headed back to the keep. "So tell me, how did you
come to be here?" Alasdair asked. "The women didna say their
names. How are they related to you?"

"Elene was a captured slave. And Isobel is our aunt," Conall
said.

Conall explained all that had happened—his father
attempting to kill the chieftain with the support of others who
hated the chieftain, but then they turned on his father and
killed him instead. Their mothers and Isobel's father dying
while fighting earlier clan battles. How Isobel had had a twin
brother who had been lost at sea. How they had befriended
Elene who had been taken prisoner before Conall and his kin
had joined the chieftain's clan and befriended her because she
was a wolf like them.

"You really have thirty wolves in your pack?" Conall asked,
sounding in awe.

"Aye, and if the five of you stay with us, that will make five
and thirty."

"I dinna know about my aunt and what she wants to do. Or
Elene. She said she'd stay with us for now, but she might want to
look for her family."

"Aye, well, you are all welcome to stay."

"I am a good hunter and a fighter," Conall said.

"And you are good at taking care of your family. That is
what's so important also in a wolf pack."

Conall nodded sagely, looking pleased at the praise. From
what Conall had told Alasdair, he had already seen so much

death in his young life. Alasdair knew he understood the impor-
tance of being there for family.

When they finally arrived at the village and the castle keep,
the outer walls still being built, he saw the two women were now
wearing *léines* and brats that made them appear as though they
were some of their own Highland women, which he was glad
for. He didn't want to have trouble with Highlanders passing
through who might cause difficulties for them because they had
Vikings living with his clan.

As soon as Elene and Isobel saw them arrive in the inner
bailey, they ran to give the bairns hugs. The young lass and lad
gave them hugs back, glad to see the women were safe. Conall
tried to look more warrior like and stiffened when Isobel and
Elene hugged him, but the women didn't seem to care. They
were just glad to see their companions safe and sound.

"We will hunt, and then eat," Alasdair said. "Bessetta is my
sister. She'll take care of the bairns if you want to hunt with us."
He meant for Elene, Isobel, and Conall to go with them if they
wanted to.

Elene said, "Some other time, if it pleases you. I'll stay with
the bairns and get to know your sister. I think they'll be more
comfortable if at least one person they know is with them."

And trust, which Alasdair understood.

"I will hunt," Isobel said, and Conall definitely wanted to
hunt, to prove he had what it took to be part of the pack.

"Did you know they have thirty wolves in the pack? With us,
five and thirty?" Conall asked Isobel.

She glanced at Alasdair for confirmation.

"Aye, if you will stay with us, that's what we'll have. It is good
that you changed your names. You've changed your garments,
but you still sound Icelandic when you speak with your distinc-
tive brogue. Which we can work on. You blend in with us other-

wise. Your nephew mistakenly said he was named Bodolf at first."

"It will take some getting used to. Dinna fault me if I dinna answer to my new name sometimes either," Isobel said.

Alasdair smiled. "Believe me, I would be the same way."

"Hey," Hans said, riding up to join them. "We have visitors. And they could be trouble. It's Baine and his brother, Cleary."

"God's wounds." They *were* trouble. And Conall was wearing Icelandic clothes still!

4

I sobel wondered if the visitors coming to see Alasdair would mean the trouble had to do with them. With her and her kin. She was thinking that she, her niece, and her nephews might fit in with this pack. After hearing their story, Alasdair's people had been kind to her and her family, even trying to help her improve her Gaelic so that no one would think she was a Viking. Providing them clothes so they appeared to be Scots too was a godsend. Though Conall needed clothes also.

"Dinna speak to anyone," Alasdair warned her and Conall. "Hans, I'll go talk to them. Keep Isobel and her nephew here."

"Aye."

But two men came riding up to greet them before Alasdair could meet them away from Isobel and Conall. Were the brothers gossipmongers who would tell anyone who would listen that the pack had taken in the enemy? Or had they suffered at the hands of the Vikings—as well they might have— and would want to kill anyone who had Norse blood?

"Alasdair," one of the men greeted him.

"Cleary," Alasdair said, inclining his head a little, then acknowledged the other man, "Baine."

"We heard you were going on a hunt. May we join you?" Cleary asked, looking over Isobel and Conall, but she didn't like the way he observed her. Then his eyes widened as he considered Conall's clothing.

"We have enough clansmen on the hunt. Another time," Alasdair said.

Cleary again eyed Isobel with speculation. "It appears you have gained some new clansmen."

Alasdair smiled at him. But it was a look that told the men to leave. That he didn't want them involved in his pack business. The two men were human so they wouldn't know Alasdair and his people were wolves then.

Alasdair told Hans, "Take Isobel and Conall on the hunt with the others. I'll join you shortly."

"Aye." Then Alasdair motioned to Isobel and her nephew to head out with them.

She was ready. So was Conall. They would take down a boar for the meal to prove they could provide for the pack, and she was eager to get out of these men's sights.

They were riding through the woods searching for game, but she still wanted to know what Alasdair would say to Cleary and Baine.

She wondered where the men were from. Probably not far from the pack's territory or they wouldn't have known they were out here hunting. Then she heard hounds barking and she wondered if they were Alasdair's. She hadn't seen them before, but she suspected they were alerting the hunters that they had found a boar. She and her nephew hurried to find the boar and helped take it down. She was elated and so was Conall.

She realized Alasdair hadn't rejoined them. She hoped the men he'd been talking to had left and wouldn't cause any difficulties. Then she saw Alasdair, and Hans joined up with him to speak with him. Pack leader business.

After they spoke, Alasdair rode up to join them and Hans was in charge of the men bringing the beast to their keep for the meal.

"Hans said you and your nephew helped to take down the boar," Alasdair said to her.

"Aye. What was the trouble with Baine and Cleary?" She wanted to know what she and her kin were up against as they rode in the direction of the keep.

"Their parents were killed by Viking raiders. They have made it a vendetta to kill any Norsemen or women they see in the Highlands."

"So we're no' safe here." Isobel figured being here was too good to be true.

"You are safe here with the pack. We wouldna give you up to the men, no matter what. You are wolves, first and foremost."

"Thank you."

"Aye. You saved a Scotswoman because she was a wolf when freeing her would have endangered you and your kin. We do the same for you and your kin."

When they arrived at the keep, he said to Hans, "You're in charge of finding work for our new pack members."

"Aye," Hans said. "Conall, you can help with building the wall." He motioned to Rory. "He'll show you what you need to do."

Then Hans left Isobel's nephew with Rory and took Isobel into the keep. "Can you cook?"

"Elene can. She's a good cook. I'm a fighter, a hunter." Aye, Isobel could cook, but she would rather fight.

Hans smiled. "If Alasdair is agreeable, you can guard the keep or the wall walk."

"Good." She was glad they wouldn't just put her to work at something she didn't know how to do or want to do.

"Your niece and younger nephew are milking the cows and gathering eggs from the chicken coops."

"They love animals."

"They do, and your younger nephew, Drummond, wants to handle the dogs."

"Will he be allowed to?" She figured someone Alasdair had trained would be the one to do that.

"Aye. We start them out young and Drummond has a real gift with the animals already."

"About the men who came to speak with Alasdair, what was that all about?" she asked Hans, wanting to know if Alasdair's brother would know anything more or would tell her more than Alasdair had done.

"Their parents had been killed in a Viking raid. You can imagine how they feel about them," Hans said.

Isobel took a deep breath. "I understand." She was just glad Elene had accepted their friendship after what had happened to her and her family.

Then Hans introduced her to the guard in charge of making assignments and he smiled. "I'm Lorne." He turned to Hans. "Dinna tell me she is looking to guard the keep. I was hoping she was seeking a husband. Me, in fact."

Hans slapped him on the back. "That's something I'll leave you to work out between the two of you." Then he left.

"Guarding the keep works for me," she said.

"Nay on being my wife, eh?"

She smiled. She knew she didn't have a chance with Alasdair, but he was the one she wanted. Someone in charge, who cared about his people, her, and her kin too. A pack leader? She would do well at leading a pack also. That's the role she had always felt she was destined to play.

~

BEFORE GLOAMING, Isobel ate with the rest of her family at a croft for this eve, but in the future, Alasdair had said he wanted them at the keep to eat their meals. For now, they were staying at the croft near a loch with the crofters, a man and his wife, Dawy and Agnes. The crofters had never been able to have bairns of their own and so they were happy to have Isobel and her family under their roof for now.

"We learned you are a guard for the keep," the man said.

"Aye." Isobel ate some of the brown bread Agnes had made. It was very good, probably even more so because they hadn't had fresh bread in so long. "The food is great."

"It is," Conall said, and she gave him a look to not eat too much.

As if Agnes realized what was not being said, she smiled. "He can eat as much as he needs. And then he can hunt for us too." She switched her attention to Isobel. "You have no guard detail tonight?"

Isobel glanced at her before she took another bite of the boar. "Nay. I am free. Did you need me to do something for you?" The crofters were generous to house so many of them at once, when Isobel and her kin were Vikings. Elene was staying in the keep with some other women. She would be sewing and doing needlework and other tasks that were required of her.

Just like Isobel would be helping to hunt for food, growing and gathering crops, and pulling guard duty. Whatever anyone needed her to assist with.

"I have it on good authority the laird is off to swim in the loch yonder—and no one will be there to guard him," Agnes said, brushing a dark strand of hair off her cheek, a twinkle in her gray-blue eyes.

Isobel was never embarrassed. Ever. Yet she felt a rush of heat fill her cheeks at once. "He probably doesna need anyone to guard him." Or he would already have assigned someone the duty.

"If anything untoward happened to him, the pack would suffer a great loss," Agnes continued, fetching more honeyed mead for Isobel.

Isobel glanced at Dawy to see his take on the situation.

"Aye, 'tis so." The dark-haired man winked at her and she felt the heat in her face renew.

"I can go," Conall said, sounding eager to get on the laird's good side.

"Nay, I will go." Isobel pulled on her brat, grabbed her sword and dagger, secured them, and seized another slice of bread. "Do as they tell you, *ja*?" She asked her kin.

"*Ja*," her nephews and niece said.

Then Isobel was out the door and striding in a hurry for the loch. She moved through the bracken when she saw Alasdair removing his sword and *sgian dubh*. Then he removed his belt, his plaid, and his shirt. Buttocks, legs, back, arms, sculpted, naked, were quite impressive. He waded into the water, and he began to swim across the loch. She was hidden in the six-foot tall bracken, watching the muscular Scot swimming, enjoying the view, the sun setting—pinks, orange, and yellow skies painting the water and him. She wondered how often he swam in the loch. It was important not to do something at a regular interval or his enemy could learn of it and be ready for him.

She was still doing her duty, listening for any sound of danger that would alert her that someone was intending to attack him, and she would stop the assassin.

All she heard was the sound of insects buzzing and the laird splashing in the water. She thought after he had finished his swim, she would take one. She had no intention of him catching her in her mission to guard him. She was still certain if he had wanted a guard, he would have assigned one.

She smiled when he finally finished his long swim and headed for shore where he'd left his clothes and weapons. But then he looked in her direction and she figured he must have smelled her scent.

Next time, if there was a next time, she would have to ensure she was downwind of him. He began to use a cloth to dry himself, his whole glorious body facing her as if he was showing off to her—which couldn't help but impress her—when he should have been turned around so he could watch for danger in the woods.

She sighed. The view was too good, and she had to remember to breathe, to listen and watch for signs of difficulty, and not be so caught up in studying the laird, for heaven's sake.

When he finished belting his plaid and securing his weapons, he headed for the keep which was southwest of her. So had he smelled her, or not?

Even if he knew she'd been out here, he probably had just been amused she had been watching him swimming in the loch. Once she no longer saw him, she moved closer to the loch and pulled off her brat, *léine*, her shoes, and then her chemise. She realized her younger niece and nephew must have bathed earlier when they were given Scottish clothes to wear because they hadn't smelled of sea salt. Whereas she and Conall had.

Then she walked into the fresh water, wading deep until she could swim. She dove under, washing the salt off her skin and out of her hair. She felt glorious. The loch was close enough to the croft and the keep that she could do this every night, though she needed Conall to take a bath too.

She floated on her back and felt at one with the silky water. She stared up at the beautiful, sparkling stars in the night's sky. She felt as though she could stay like this forever. But then Conall howled from the croft, telling her she needed to retire to bed and get some sleep. She wanted to turn into her wolf and bite him!

~

WHEN ALASDAIR HAD FINISHED his swim, feeling invigorated, he had been ready to dress and return to the keep. But then he had smelled Isobel's delightful scent in the direction of the bracken. Unable to help himself, he'd dressed and watched for any sign of her, but she'd been hidden, and he couldn't see her in the tall plants. He thought of walking through the bracken to locate her, but then he assumed she'd only been there to bathe and when she'd seen him in the loch, she had waited until he left.

He had headed back to the keep, but then he had detoured to see what she was up to. When he had seen her strip off her clothes and enter the loch, he'd been intrigued—so much so, he couldn't pull his gaze away from the sight of her.

Toned muscles, beautiful breasts, long blond hair unbound, and a body that looked to be perfect to share carnal pleasure with and carry a Scotsman's bairn. His bairn even.

But when she began floating on her back, observing the stars as if she was a water sprite of the loch, he couldn't move, his groin tightening, and he had the greatest urge to join her.

A wolf inside the croft howled. A young male wolf, probably Conall.

Then she turned as if she'd smelled Alasdair this time—the breeze switching back and forth across the loch, so mayhap she had. She stared at him, looking shocked to see him observing her. He smiled. He thought of leaving, of giving her some privacy, but wolves shifted naked in front of each other so it wasn't that uncommon to see each other in that way. Though they were new to each other and he was more than intrigued.

"If you are there to guard me, you need no' do so any longer. I'm quite clean now and coming out."

"If I had known you wanted to bathe, I would have allowed you to go first," he said, not budging from his spot of claimed territory—right next to her clothes.

"I was here to guard you."

He raised a brow. "Lorne sent you to guard me?" Now that surprised him. Lorne never sent anyone to watch over Alasdair because he didn't want anyone having to pull the duty. Though sometimes Hans or Rory came with him to provide some extra security and take turns swimming also.

Isobel swam closer to the shore, but she wasn't getting out. "Nay, Dawy and Agnes did."

He glanced back at the croft. "Did they now?" He swung his attention back to Isobel.

"*Ja*. Aye. Then when you left, or pretended to leave, I wanted to wash off the sea salt on my skin and hair. Dinna fault them for it."

"Quite the contrary. I'm glad they sent you to me. How are you liking it here so far?"

She smiled and left the water then when he wouldn't leave. "We are very happy." She was like a water goddess—divine to behold, the water dripping from her glorious skin. On the shore, she grabbed up her chemise and pulled it on, the sheer fabric clinging to her wet skin, her nipples extended, her short blond curls between her legs catching his eye.

Then she pulled her léine on, fastened her brat, and secured her weapons. He walked her back to the croft.

"You truly are no' going to scold them for sending me out to guard you?" she asked, sounding so serious, he chuckled.

"Nay. They are a kindhearted couple who were delighted that you and your kin would stay with them." He inclined his head to her when they reached the door, but he didn't leave, wanting to kiss her in the worst way. Would a Norsewoman's lips be as sweet as a Scotswoman's? He was dying to learn the truth.

She opened the door and bid him a good night, then shut the door. He stared after it wishing he'd kissed her and not allowed her to get away. He let out his breath and told himself tomorrow would be another day, and tomorrow eve at gloaming? Mayhap another encounter with the Viking water goddess?

When he retired to bed that night, all he could think of was Isobel—and how much he had wanted to seduce the woman from the moment he had laid eyes on her when he was a wolf in the woods while she had climbed the cliff.

He finally drifted off to sleep until he was swept away into the world of dreams.

Hans bumped his shoulder. "If you make a play for her and she and her pack kill you, we will take down every last one of them." He spoke his words only so Alasdair could hear them.

"You will no'. If she and her pack see me as a threat, I will retreat until she realizes I'm no' going away. But if she did try to kill me and somehow succeeded, you would take no action against her or her kin. They are only trying to survive, just like we are."

The wolves' ears were perked, listening to any sounds of danger or something to hunt.

"You are the most stubborn of us, Alasdair."

"I need a wolf mate. She will do." Finding another wolf pack was nigh to impossible. Wolves, aye, but not lupus garous like them. She intrigued him because she was not a Highland lass, but from the north country.

Their other brother Rory, and their sister, Bessetta, joined them and he wanted to groan out loud. Did they have to follow him everywhere? Aye, he was the eldest, by about fifteen minutes, and by virtue of that, he'd taken charge from the time of birth on. He'd scrambled to his mother's teat and once he'd had his fill, he'd ensured his smaller sister, the last born, had plenty of milk too. It had been a good thing he had taken charge of his siblings from the onset because once their mother and father had died at sea ten years later, he and his siblings had been fending for themselves. Until he took over the pack.

"I want the one with the black fur on his tail," Bessetta said.

Rory scoffed. "He is a wild Norseman. And too young for you."

"And Alasdair is intrigued with the Norsewoman. She is as wild as the wolf with the black-tipped tail. Besides, you are a wild Highlander." Bessetta and the others quickly crouched lower when one of the wolves looked their way.

Because of the direction the wind was blowing, the northern wolves couldn't smell them, but Alasdair and his siblings smelled them.

"Does she always hunt with her bow?" Bessetta asked Alasdair. "Have you seen her as a wolf?"

"Aye." A beautiful wolf with a mix of white, yellowish, and black fur, her chin and throat white.

"Alasdair, are you going to sleep your life away?" Hans was asking him, and Alasdair opened his eyes and glanced around his chamber, realizing that the sun was already streaming through one of the narrow windows. "We worried you were ill. Are you feeling all right?"

Alasdair didn't even know what Isobel and her kin looked like while wearing their wolf coats. The dream he'd had of her was already fading, yet he recalled vividly what she had looked like. The dreams he'd had of her before? Those had come true. Would these also? Well, not about how they had met. Or that he had to take her as a mate. Even Elene could be a good choice for a mate. She had a real infinity for bairns and sewing. Though Isobel was really good with the bairns also. She was protective and eager to show her fighting and hunting skills. For her to take charge of a group of bairns and a slave and cross the dangerous ocean to hopefully find a safe home for them when they were moving into the enemies' territory? She was remarkable.

He had hopelessly fallen for her.

"Conall said Isobel was at the loch guarding you," Hans said as Alasdair hurried to dress.

He sighed. He hadn't thought that news would get out. "She wanted to bathe in the loch."

"Aye, because of the journey they'd made here. Conall bathed this morning. You came into the keep late, later than usual last eve. I was afraid I'd have to send men out after you. That some harm might have come to you." Hans smiled as they headed down the winding stairs to the great hall to break their fast, appearing as though he didn't believe anything of the sort.

"Did you?" Alasdair hadn't considered that, but it would be protocol to check up on him if he were late in returning for the night when he'd been alone. Or so he'd thought at the time.

"Aye. Just Rory and me though."

Alasdair shook his head. So that's how they knew he had been swimming at the loch near the croft. The other loch was closer to the keep and he suspected they had wanted to see if he was planning to visit Isobel at the croft instead.

"When Rory and I saw the reason for your delay, we left the two of you alone. Though I had a devil of a time getting Rory to come with me without making a big scene and alerting you we were there."

"After I swam?" Alasdair asked.

"Aye."

He shook his head again. He couldn't believe his brothers had arrived at the loch also but had to have been downwind of him and Isobel and said nary a word of it to him. Until now.

"If you are no' interested in the lass, I would be willing to mate her. Most of the members of the pack would, to be sure. Rory's tongue was hanging out the rest of the eve."

Alasdair laughed.

"'Tis true. He will deny it, but what I say is true. Did you want to change the seating arrangements when we break our fast this morn?"

"Why?" Alasdair asked, suspecting he knew what his brother was getting at.

"So she can sit beside you? She can be your personal guard."

"Nay." Alasdair wouldn't mind being *her* personal guard and protecting her sweet body all night long. But he knew if he had her sit beside him, the word would circulate throughout the pack that he had already selected her to be his mate when he needed to get to know her better first.

5

That morning when they went to break their fast, Isobel noticed the change in people's attitude toward her. More deferent. She wasn't sure what it meant.

"Och," Elene said, "you wouldna believe what everyone is saying."

"What?"

"That you swam with his lairdship in the loch last night." Elene's eyes were wide. "Did you?"

"We are sitting at the lower table, *ja*? If Alasdair and I were seeing each other as in courting as wolves, wouldn't I be sitting at the high table?" At least Isobel thought so.

Elene shrugged. "I have no idea. So tell me. Is it true?"

"Nay. I washed off the sea salt coating my skin and hair."

"Oh, aye. I did too. It felt wonderful. I made the bairns bathe. They fought me over it. Though once they were clean, they were grateful. The salt was so harsh on their skin. But I have heard tell that his lairdship was at the loch at the same time as you last eve."

Isobel smiled. "I was guarding him."

"Nay." Then Elene laughed. "That is precious. Three women

in the clan are ready to kill you over it. They have been trying to catch his eye since their families joined the pack. Just watch out for them."

Isobel choked on her mead and once she caught her breath, she laughed. She didn't think she stood a chance to be Alasdair's mate, but she loved a challenge. "They will have no chance with him." If they had, she figured he wouldn't have been eyeing her so at the loch last night. He probably would have already mated one of them.

"Who are they? Since I am no' staying at the keep, I am no' privy to what is going on there." Which in a way was kind of nice. On the other hand, it was nice having Elene there who could tell her what was being said.

"Mege is the one who is pushing her plan the most. The pretty dark-haired woman seated two tables over. She is glowering at you even now as we speak. Then there is Marioziota and Theebet. But they willna pursue Alasdair unless he does the pursuing. Mege isna one to cross, however. She thought she had an in with him and then you came along. Alasdair's sister has filled me in on all the details."

"What about you?" Isobel thought that Elene would stand a good chance with Alasdair, even better than she would because Elene was Scottish.

Elene laughed. "I have an eye on one of Alasdair's brothers. No' that either take any interest in me, but you definitely have caught the laird's eye. I think it was when you practically shouted at Alasdair that there had been no one on the beach with us that had intrigued him most of all."

Isobel sighed. "I hadna meant to make the outburst. He immediately knew I was a Viking and that there were others on the beach then."

"And once he learned who they were, he respected you for trying to protect them."

Isobel looked askance at Elene. "So which brother are you interested in?"

Elene laughed. "I willna say unless things change between us. By then, I'm sure you'll know yourself."

Lorne stalked into the great hall to speak with Alasdair. Everyone quieted and Isobel figured a problem had arisen.

Isobel wondered if she would be needed to help other guards in defense of the keep. She admired the clan for building the wall around the keep, but they still had a long way to go to make it fully secure. She thought she could help build it when she wasn't doing guard duty.

As much as everyone was watching Alasdair and Lorne, she knew it must be serious.

Alasdair glanced at her, his look stern. Was the trouble over *her*?

～

ALASDAIR KNEW he was going to have to ultimately deal with Cleary and Baine one way or another. They wanted to join his prosperous clan. They couldn't unless they were wolves. Turning them meant they would have difficulty controlling their shifting during the full moon and couldn't shift at all during the new moon. Those who had fewer human roots were known as royals and could shift at will at any time they wished. Which made him wonder if Isobel was a royal wolf or not.

"They came with a cache of fish," Lorne said. "Do I accept the fish and send them away?"

"They are trying to learn if Isobel and her kin are from the north."

"Aye. They've tried every way they can to ingratiate themselves to the pack," Hans said. "I say we turn them and make them part of the pack."

"What about Isobel and her nephews and niece? If we turn Cleary and Baine and they become part of the pack, I still believe they will want them dead because the Vikings killed their family," Alasdair said. The men were likeable, hard workers. He didn't want to eliminate them, and they were good hunters, fighters—and fishermen, it seemed. But he couldn't allow them to harm anyone in his pack.

"They can help build the fortifications," Rory said. "And if they try to harm the Vikings, we'll eliminate the troublemakers. You know they're not going to stop trying to join our clan, and at the same time, learn if Isobel and her kin are Vikings."

"I agree. Thank them for the fish. Ask them to join us for the meal. Beyond that, they can become part of our clan and they can help build our wall, among other things. They'll stay in the barracks with the rest of the men and eat with us during the meals. But make room at a table farthest from Isobel and her kin," Alasdair said.

"Aye, we will." Rory hurried off to have some of their people make room at one of the lower tables and Lorne went to fetch Cleary and Baine.

As soon as the men entered the great hall, Lorne seated them at the only table that had space available on one of the benches. Both men thanked Alasdair then began to eat and drink the food and ale that women brought out for them.

"When do we turn them?" Hans asked, knowing Alasdair had decided to do so or he wouldn't have had the humans dining with them or joining the clan.

"Get a good day's work out of them building the wall. Tonight, in the barracks, you and I can take care of them." Alasdair ate some of his venison. He and his eldest brother would take responsibility for the men and if they went rogue, he would take care of them. He wouldn't leave that up to the rest of his pack.

"Aye."

They tried to never turn anyone unless they had no choice—that someone had accidentally bitten a human, or that a human had seen one of their kind shifting. Then they would have to either eliminate them or turn them. Because there were so few wolves, they didn't just eliminate them unless they couldn't do otherwise. As in a case where they were members of an enemy clan and would not live peaceably with his people if they were turned.

There were advantages to being one of their kind—increased longevity, faster healing powers, and of course, their heightened wolf senses. For newly turned wolves, the shifting issues were the problem. Neither of the men had any family, so that helped Alasdair in making the decision to turn them.

Alasdair watched the two men as they entered the great hall with Lorne and were escorted to their table. Actually everyone did. Cleary and Baine glanced around the room until they spied Isobel. When they saw her, they observed her. Alasdair hadn't figured they would show that much interest in her—unless they assumed the worst of her.

Alasdair told Rory, "Hans and I will turn them tonight in the barracks. We want to have other men on hand if we should have trouble with them. And they must be disarmed."

"Aye. They are already showing way too much interest in Isobel. Do you think 'tis because she is so bonny?" Rory asked.

Why hadn't Alasdair thought of that? He'd been thinking the men had heard Isobel and her kin were Vikings and staying with his clan now. Mayhap their interest in her went in that direction instead.

"We will keep an eye on them. Mayhap, once they are wolves, they'll understand we're all wolves under one roof and we're here for each other. If they canna live with the rules, we'll have no choice but to eliminate them. If we dinna turn them to see if they come around, I'm afraid they'll target them when we're least expecting it. If they are only interested in the lass because of how comely she is, they could still turn on her once they learn she's not a Scotswoman. We'll have to have eyes on them at all times." Alasdair thought of the bairns playing in the meadow, or Conall and Isobel with them on the hunt and *accidentally* being killed. Or that Isobel might bathe in the loch again on her own and the brothers could catch her at it. But Alasdair certainly thought of her and her kind being in danger where these men were concerned unless turning them changed their outlook.

Rory had purposefully made sure Cleary and Baine were sitting next to Lorne. He would listen in on anything that was being said. Alasdair wished he could listen in on their conversations himself. Until Cleary and Baine had arrived, he had been concentrating on Isobel smiling and chatting it up easily with Elene. They appeared to be the best of friends. Isobel had been slow at making friends among his people, though the crofters loved her and her family already and wanted to keep them there for as long as they wanted to stay with them. His sister, Bessetta, had tried to befriend Isobel also. He hadn't heard how that was working out. Bessetta was sitting at the head table with him, as she should be, and she hadn't said she wanted to sit by Isobel. He was hoping they'd become good friends.

Isobel's younger nephew and her niece seemed happy to be with the other bairns of the pack. Bairns were more resilient, and the bairns in his pack were good about welcoming more wolf bairns in their ranks. He'd seen them playing in the gardens as wolves already. He'd also seen them doing the chores without complaint and he hadn't seen any fights break out among them—yet.

Conall seemed to be fitting in. When he wasn't working on the wall, he was practicing fighting with the other youth his age.

He appeared to have made a couple of friends. Alasdair was glad for that. Elene seemed to fit in with the other women and from what others had told him, she hadn't said anything about leaving the clan to find her other pack members, if any of them were still alive. They would help her to locate them when they were able to.

First, though, he wanted to get the fortifications done on the wall, to make it more secure before they left the keep for any length of time. Alasdair kept worrying about Cleary and Baine, though he knew everyone would be keeping an eye on them.

That evening, Alasdair went to speak to Isobel to ensure that she understood what was going on with Cleary and Baine before she heard it from anyone else.

They were in the meadow alone together and he said, "We have Cleary and Baine under watch at all times. Hans and I are turning them tonight."

"They'll have more control over their shifting right now."

"Aye, between the full moon and new, they will. Which is partly why I wanted to do it now, but mostly because they seem to be interested in you and your kin and I canna have them giving you trouble. They've always wanted to join the clan, but since they're no' wolves, I couldna allow it before."

Isobel bit her lip, and he tenderly rubbed her chin. "Mayhap I am mistaken, and they are only interested in you. But I couldna have that either."

She raised her brows. "Nay."

He smiled. "'Tis possible."

"I doubt it. I imagine 'tis more likely that they believe we're from the north and they would like to destroy us. They saw the way Conall was dressed when we were on the earlier hunt."

"We hope turning them will change their opinion once they learn the truth about you and your family, but if it doesna and they wish to harm you, we'll take care of them."

"Thank you, but if they come after us and I'm there, I'll protect my kin."

"You have all of us for that from now on." He suspected it would take a while before she believed his kind, who were not Vikings, would take care of her and her kin.

She nodded, but he sensed she felt she still must take care of her own family—as if it were her destiny.

"I'm going to the barracks with Hans now and take care of this little matter. If you have any trouble at all, just let me or my brothers know."

"*Ja.*"

"Aye," he corrected her, not wanting her to make the slip in front of someone other than their pack members. But he knew from the expression on her face she intended to take matters into her own hands if either man threatened her or her kin. He didn't blame her, though he wanted to take care of them himself to prove to her that he was good for his word.

"Will I see you this eve?" she asked.

He smiled. "Do you mean will I go swimming again this eve?"

"I'll be there to guard you. You shouldna be alone like that. And I'm a guard."

He chuckled. "The same for you." He saw Hans coming and he knew he wanted to get this over with. "Are you ready?"

"Aye." Hans inclined his head to Isobel. "Are you, Alasdair?"

"Aye." Alasdair slapped him on the back. "I will see you later, Isobel." Then he headed for the barracks with Hans.

"You told her?" Hans asked.

"Aye. I wanted her to know she and her family are safe with us."

"Is she safe with *you*?"

Alasdair chuckled. "Perfectly."

"Bessetta has said the woman has caught your eye. She

notices things, you know."

"She's a wolf. Sometimes she notices too much."

Hans smiled. But when they arrived at the barracks, a group of his pack members were talking to Cleary and Baine, and they all grew quiet, knowing just what Alasdair and Hans planned to do.

Before Alasdair and Hans could strip off their clothes, two wolves barged into the barracks. He didn't recognize them at first, but then he smelled their scents. Isobel and Conall. They raced into the barracks and attacked Cleary and Baine, not viciously, but biting them as the brothers threw their arms up to protect themselves. The wolves' bites broke the skin, and then Isobel and Conall turned and ran out the door.

If they had turned the brothers, Cleary and Baine were now of Viking wolf ancestry. Alasdair wasn't sure if that was the reason for Isobel turning the men so that they wouldn't kill them if they knew they were now related. Or she just didn't trust Alasdair and his people to turn Cleary and Baine and keep her and her kin safe.

Shocked didn't cover how Alasdair felt about Isobel and her nephew turning Cleary and Baine. Both men were holding their arms, looking just as stunned as everyone else there. Once the Viking wolves disappeared into the night, everyone looked at Alasdair to see what he wanted to do about it.

"Your—your hounds attacked us," Cleary said, sounding astounded. "We didna provoke them, I swear. We're always good with animals."

Good. Because they were among lots of wolves that they needed to get along with. Especially the Viking wolves.

"We'll talk in the morn when we break our fast," Alasdair said, needing to speak at once with Isobel. He would have no wolf under his rule making his or her own plans without his agreement. Turning men that Alasdair had welcomed into the pack could not be allowed. But then he added, "Unless you need to discuss matters with them as they play out, Lorne."

Lorne would oversee the men who would watch the newly turned wolves. If they had been turned, Lorne might need to explain what had happened to them. But if they didn't shift until daybreak, there was no sense in trying to explain it to them until then.

"I will see you in the morn. Though if there is any trouble"— more so than what Isobel and Conall had pulled—"come and see me." Then Alasdair and Hans left the barracks.

Alasdair was headed straight for the crofters' farm by the loch to speak with the Viking woman when he realized Hans was sticking with him. "You dinna need to be with me for this. Go. Get your rest. I'll be returning to my chamber shortly."

"Dinna be too angry with her. She only wanted to protect her kin," Hans said.

"Do you think I dinna know that? How does it look to the clan when a woman—a Norsewoman—takes it upon herself to turn the Scots without my permission in front of all of us?"

"Like she was protecting her kin."

"Dinna stick up for her."

"I am only saying that's how our people will view it."

"I was going to turn them. Well, you and me. It's our responsibility, no' hers. Does she think she can protect her family better than we can?"

"She lost her uncle and the rest of her family. She's had to do so much on her own to keep her niece and nephews safe for weeks on end."

Alasdair growled. "Didna I tell you to return to the keep?" Was no one going to listen to his orders any more now that the woman had arrived?

"I was thinking of swimming in the loch."

Alasdair looked sharply at his brother.

Hans smiled at him, then frowned again. "She and her kin fled a certain death from her own kind. She was responsible for their safety on a long and perilous journey when two of the five of them are but bairns. She would do anything to protect them, dinna you see?"

Alasdair rubbed his whiskered chin.

"Mayhap you should wait until morn to speak with her."

"Nay. You think I willna hold my temper when speaking with her?" Even now as Alasdair walked briskly across the land toward the crofters' home, he had lost some of his anger. All he had to see was the loch in the distance and think of the naked Icelander who made him want her like no other lass had ever done.

"I think you are still angry with her. After we learned the two of you were at the loch last night, I spread the word that everyone must use the one in the south from now on. 'Tis closer to the keep anyway."

Alasdair let out his breath. "I will watch my words with her. But I'm no' pleased with their actions this eve and I canna guarantee that I willna"—he ground his teeth—"I will try to keep my temper. Go back to the keep and watch things for me, will you? It won't be long before everyone knows what happened at the barracks and I need you to quell the unrest if our people are afraid of the Norsewoman's uncalled actions." She was ultimately responsible for the attack because he knew her nephew wouldn't have done it on his own.

"Aye. I will see you in the morn then, unless there's trouble before then." Hans turned around and walked back in the direction of the keep.

Alasdair charged ahead, wanting to get this over with and hoping he could keep his temper in check. He didn't remember a time when anyone countermanded his authority in such a manner before. He wouldn't allow it.

6

"Y ou did what?" Agnes, the crofter's wife, asked Isobel, sounding alarmed when she learned that Isobel and her oldest nephew had turned Cleary and Baine without the pack leader's permission.

"I had to do it." Isobel knew they'd probably be thrown off the lands now, but she felt with all her heart that she'd had no choice. Just like she'd had no choice but to take her family across the ocean for weeks on end and put them in so much danger. Staying with the clan could have been their death sentence anyway. As much as people had talked about them being outsiders and traitors, she had been certain the chieftain would have ended their lives there. "One of the men who was pulling guard duty with me said that Cleary and his brother were trying to learn who we were. Where we were from. He said we were so fair haired, he was afraid that Vikings had infiltrated the clan and Alasdair was unaware of the danger we posed to him and your people. I take full responsibility for what I've done. Conall only went along with it because he knew I couldn't manage two men on my own. He should not be punished for my actions."

Conall said, "Nay, Isobel. I did it to protect my siblings also. If you had not done it yourself, I would have."

"He will be coming for you then," Agnes said, worried, wringing her hands, glancing at the floor where the younger bairns were sound asleep on blanket-covered straw beds.

Isobel knew she wouldn't want to part with the bairns. Agnes loved them like they were her own bairns that she'd never been able to have.

"I dinna want to see you go," Agnes said, tears filling her eyes. She straightened her posture. "I will tell Alasdair that I begged you to turn Cleary and Baine to ensure the little ones remained safe."

Dawy shook his head. "Alasdair will know the truth. No one gets anything past him."

"I wouldna have you take the blame," Isobel said. She would take the blame for her niece and nephews should they have gotten themselves in trouble, but she would never allow anyone to take the blame for her own actions.

"Alasdair is coming," Conall warned as he watched out the window.

"You stay here," Isobel said to him, knowing he'd want to come with her and speak his own mind. But she thought she might be able to smooth things over with Alasdair if she went alone.

"You didna make me do it, Isobel," Conall said. "And I will take responsibility for my own actions."

She was proud of him for doing what was right. Though she still wanted to protect him. His siblings needed him.

"Let me speak with him alone first," she said, not wanting her nephew to have to deal with the angry laird. She headed outside to intercept Alasdair before he was within wolf hearing distance of the croft, though she suspected Agnes and Dawy and her nephew would be watching out the window. Conall would come to her rescue if this led to a physical fight between her and Alasdair. She didn't know the laird well enough to know how he was going to react.

"What were you thinking?" Alasdair asked as he and Isobel continued to close the gap between them.

"That Cleary and Baine would try to hurt us still if they were Scottish wolves," Isobel said.

"You couldna ask me what I thought of the matter first?"

"I thought over what some of the guardsmen said to me and I had to do this."

"You know what this cost us?"

"Your pride?"

Alasdair scoffed, though to an extent she figured he knew she was right. "What if my people feel you are as untrustworthy as Cleary and Baine? Dangerous to their well-being even?"

"I had to protect my family. Besides, if I had come to you and asked if it wouldna be better if I turned them, would you have allowed me to?"

"I would have seriously considered your suggestion."

"But would you have said aye?"

"Nay. As the pack leader, it's my duty to turn people if the circumstances warrant. It's on my conscience. What if this doesna work out as you planned? What if they are even angrier that Viking wolves turned them? Had you even considered that possibility?"

"Aye, I did. And if they want to fight me, so be it."

Alasdair shook his head.

"What do you want me to say or do?" She folded her arms. "I willna apologize."

Alasdair almost smiled, but he was still frowning.

"We will leave here if you tell us to," she added.

"You canna. No' with the little ones and the problems you would face as Vikings and further as wolves in a strange land."

"What must I do to make this right?"

Alasdair looked so sternly at her, she wondered just what he was thinking. A stay in the dungeon for a time for her disobedience? "You and Conall will each take one of the wolves in hand and have to supervise them for several hours during the day when you are not doing your normal duties."

"Aye. And at night?"

Alasdair raised a brow. "They will stay in the barracks and others will watch over them. Have you turned anyone before?"

"Nay."

He let out his breath on a heavy sigh. "You will have your work cut out for you. Take care that you do not decide to do anything further to this extent before you have been told to do it."

"Aye." Isobel couldn't believe the laird was letting them off so easily. She suspected the rest of the clan may not be so generous with them on the morrow. She was sure the word had spread throughout the pack already about what they'd done.

Then Alasdair bid her a good night and turned and headed back to the keep. She watched him go, tall, handsome, the kind of braw man who would suit her disposition well. He hadn't punished her and her nephew like he could have. Not really. She smiled and headed back to the croft.

Even the little ones were at the windows now. Conall opened the door. "Are we banished?"

"Nay."

"Well, what then?" Conall asked.

"We have to watch Cleary and Baine when we're not performing our other duties."

"That could be punishment enough," Conall said and ushered his siblings back to bed.

Isobel and the others breathed in a tentative sigh of relief.

Who knew how it would be on the morrow when they broke their fast in the morn?

⁓

WHEN ALASDAIR REACHED THE KEEP, both his brothers and his sister were waiting to hear how it went.

"I hope you didna give her too much grief," Bessetta said. "As a warrior, she will be a good fighter, dinna you think?"

"It wasna her place to deal with the brothers. That's all I'll say on the matter, except that she and Conall are to watch the brothers when their own duty is done."

"Aye," Hans said. "It will be done."

"Not everyone will like that you are no' punishing them further," Rory said. "What do we say about it?"

"Naught about it at all. My decision stands. Why are you not abed?" Then he went to his chamber and shut the door. The woman would be his undoing.

⁓

EARLY THE NEXT MORN, Alasdair arrived at the great hall to see his people bustling to get the food on the trestle tables and everyone there grew quiet when he walked in. He first looked for Isobel. He couldn't help himself. The woman fascinated him to no end, and he hoped his people wouldn't give her or her nephew grief for her actions last night. To his surprise, both Cleary and Baine were seated between her and her nephew Conall.

The men were silent and when Alasdair's brothers joined him at the high table, Hans said, "I spoke with Lorne earlier this morn and he said that Isobel and her nephew came to the barracks and took the brothers in hand. You said you told them that when they weren't working, they were to watch the brothers."

"Aye."

"I just wanted to confirm that with you."

"Aye, that's what I said. Good. At least they are doing what they were told to do. Did Cleary and Baine shift last night?"

"Aye, for a short while. They headed straight for the croft where Isobel and her kin are staying. They just stared at the croft, pawed at the ground a bit, circled it a couple of times, but they didn't seem aggressive as in they wanted to kill Isobel or her nephew for turning them. Five of our men were with them as wolves and they finally turned them around and herded them back to the barracks where they slept the rest of the night and woke in their human skin this morn," Hans said.

"Did you speak with them, or did Lorne, about visiting the croft?" Alasdair asked, concerned that the brothers wished to harm the Vikings.

"I spoke to them and asked why they had gone to the croft that morn. They said they couldn't help themselves. They didn't know why. I dinna know if they were lying or if they truly dinna know why they did it. With turning into wolves, it's a big adjustment to make in their lives. Of course, we talked to them about everything after they turned. And several of us went running with them to make sure they didn't do anything they shouldn't— like kill our livestock or threaten anyone or even just run away."

"All right. We'll have to watch them for any behavior that seems dangerous." Then Alasdair and his people ate their meal before they went off to do their duties. He admired Isobel for doing what he'd told her she had to do. Though he hadn't expected to see her eating with them at the lower table. Anyone could have watched them then.

Before he left the keep, he was dying to know what Isobel had been talking to the two men about though. They had been listening to her, but not once had they said anything in response. He wondered if she'd known they were at the croft last night as wolves. Then he suspected she had since she would have smelled their scents.

But then Isobel was pulling guard duty on the walls that were complete and looking out to the woods and pastureland for any signs of trouble. Rory had put Cleary and Baine on the section of the wall that needed to be finished. Conall was also out there helping with the wall.

While Alasdair was in the inner bailey taking stock of things, Bessetta came out to see him. "Do you know what Isobel was saying to Cleary and Baine?"

"Nay. I did see that they were no' saying anything in return." Though he couldn't help but be curious about what was said.

"Cleary said that Isobel told them if they came to the croft again as wolves in the middle of the night, to howl and she would see to them."

"See to them?" Alasdair was at once concerned that she meant to tear into them. Though wolves had to sometimes to set boundaries with other wolves. It didn't mean she meant to kill them.

"Aye. I dinna know what she meant. Greet them? Fight them? I thought you should know so you can speak to Isobel and make sure she doesn't get herself into any further trouble." Bessetta smiled at him. "She's up on the wall walk. No one else is around. Mayhap now would be a good time. Eh?"

"Aye. Do you no' have any work today?" He knew she had, and he didn't have to remind her of it, but he didn't want her watching him when he spoke with Isobel.

"Och, too much work to do," Bessetta said cheerily, brushing a stray hair out of her face, smiled again, turned on her heel, and went inside.

Bessetta was not one to gossip, but she seemed to like Isobel and she appeared to want to ensure that Isobel didn't do anything further that would get her in trouble with him or his people. He appreciated that. He headed up the curved stairs of the westernmost tower and when he reached the wall walk, he made his way to where Isobel was watching the land.

She turned when she either heard his approach or smelled his scent, or both.

"Thank you for taking care of the men this morning when we broke our fast," he said.

"They came to me."

Now that surprised Alasdair. He thought for certain she had told them they had to sit with her as part of her assigned duty. "Oh?"

"Aye. Conall and I watched them earlier, but we did not invite them to sit with us at the meal. I thought mayhap you had sent them to sit between Conall and me."

Alasdair frowned. "Nay. I thought you had asked them to sit there."

"Mayhap one of your brothers did. Or Lorne."

He was certain they wouldn't have. "What was discussed?"

"They didn't talk, so I did. I was surprised they wouldn't have a lot to say since they had to have known we turned them."

He nodded. "So what did *you* say to them?"

"I told them all about the joy of being wolves. The good things, and the not so good. But I'm sure your people had already explained that to them."

"And about you taking it upon yourself to bite Cleary and your nephew biting Baine?"

"I told him that wolves with Viking blood are far superior to Scots' wolves. That they would thank me for giving them some of my roots." She smiled at Alasdair.

He closed his gaping mouth. "Superior."

"Aye." Isobel's smile was charming and mischievous at the same time, he thought.

"Dinna tell the rest of my people that." He leaned out against the wall and watched the land himself. He was proud of what they'd taken over and wanted to keep these lands safe for him and his pack.

"I've heard it said there are several newcomers to the pack—female wolves of an eligible age who have joined with their families—who are eager to mate you," Isobel said.

"I havena noticed." He was surprised she'd bring that up.

"I know we live extraordinarily long lives, but wouldn't it benefit the pack if you found a wife among them, mated her, and began to have some bairns? I have counted only five in the pack. Well, and my niece and nephew make seven."

"What did you say to Cleary and Baine about going to the croft at the loch where you and your kin are staying?" Alasdair had every intention of keeping the conversation on the matter he wanted to discuss with her, not about rumors concerning his finding a mate.

"Ahh," she said, and turned her attention to the lands stretching out before them. "That I will come out and greet them, if they howled to let me know they have come to see me."

"Why did they go to see you?"

"You havena asked them? I think it would be easy to assume they wanted to know more about their newfound Viking heritage. As you might have seen, they didn't say anything to me, just listened while we were eating."

"We asked them why they had gone to the croft, but they wouldna say. Either they don't really understand why they went out there, or they didna want to admit why they had gone to see you," Alasdair said.

"As in they were ready to fight me? I would have put them in their place. No' killed them. But showed them, like an alpha wolf would, that they had a place in the pack and trying to take me down—if that had been their intent—wouldna have worked."

He rubbed his chin in thought. "If they go to your place again and dinna have an escort like they did last eve, you howl, and I will take care of them."

"Will your people think you are siding with the wild Vikings in your midst? Some of them call us that, you know."

"Who?"

"The women who wish for you to mate them. Mayhap their family's position would be elevated if their daughter mated you. Some try to whisper behind my back but Elene or your sister hear. Some are bolder about it."

"Dinna fight them over it," he warned. It was one thing to turn men who might have caused them difficulties even if the Vikings had not showed up, but to injure a woman in his pack who had his protection, that was not the same.

She shrugged. "I care no' for the bitter words these women— or men—speak, but if I am attacked physically, that is another story. And I willna howl for anyone to come and protect me. I will protect myself and anyone else who may need protecting."

He should be frustrated with her. She was unlike any woman he'd ever met. Yet, he was attracted to her strength and fierce pride and her determination to protect those who needed protection. "Are you on guard duty tonight?"

"Nay, I will be watching over Cleary and Baine though."

"No' at night. They will be in the barracks and the men there will watch them. You will guard me while I swim in the loch." Last night he had been too angered by what she had done. But he had regretted not seeing her swim.

She smiled. "It would be my pleasure. I mean, honor." She inclined her head and continued to watch for signs of trouble when he wanted her to pay attention to him!

Was he mad? She was doing her assigned duties.

"This eve then." Though he would see her during the nooning meal and the one this evening, he couldn't speak to her during the meals. Not when she was sitting at a lower table, and he was sitting at the high table. But who had made Cleary and Baine sit with her and her nephew then?

When he reached the stairs, he ran down them to the bottom and then stalked across the inner bailey to speak with Cleary and Baine while they were building the wall. "A word with the two of you, but you can continue to work."

"Aye," the brothers said.

Conall glanced in their direction, looking curious about what was about to be said, but he continued to work as well.

"You went to the croft by the loch last night. Why?" Alasdair asked.

"To stretch our legs as wolves. We were driven to do it," Cleary said.

"By why in that direction? Why not toward the other loch that is closer, or the woods, or just anywhere? Why there?"

"She scared us half to death. We didn't know it was her and her nephew who bit us. But we...we had to follow the scent trail of the wolves that bit us. We had to know who turned us," Cleary said.

"And?"

"Naught else. We were...just driven to learn who."

Alasdair wasn't sure that was all there was to it. He glanced at Baine, but he just nodded as if agreeing with everything his older brother said. "Who told you to sit between Isobel and Conall at the meal this morn?"

"Mege," both Cleary and Baine said at the same time.

"Mege?" She didn't make seating arrangements or make any decisions of that magnitude. But then Alasdair realized she had made overtures that she was interested in mating him if he was interested back. Mayhap she thought if she told the men to sit with the Vikings, trouble would ensue, and Isobel would get herself into difficulties with Alasdair.

"Aye," Cleary said. "We thought it was because we went to the croft where Isobel and Conall were staying, and Isobel would want to tell us off."

"Did she?" Alasdair asked.

"Nay. She was really nice about everything. She told us what we can expect as wolves and she said that as Viking wolves would we be even more—" Cleary paused, his eyes widening, as if he realized what he was going to say probably wouldn't set well with the Highland clan chief.

"Superior to our own kind?" Alasdair offered.

"Aye, but we know she is wrong."

Alasdair swore he heard Conall snicker. "We are equals as wolves no matter who might have bitten you." But Alasdair would have his sister say something to Mege about involving herself in seating arrangements.

"It was all right that we sat with them at the meal, was it no'?" Baine asked. "We enjoyed their company."

"You said no' a word." Alasdair couldn't understand it.

Both Baine and Cleary's ears turned red.

"They are both smitten with my aunt," Conall said. "But they're also cowed by her. She told them to say what they felt, but they were afraid to."

"We were no' afraid," Cleary said, angry now.

But Alasdair could tell that was the case already. "Work hard on the wall. You're doing good work so far." Alasdair had no intention of having the two brothers, who were smitten with Isobel, sit with her further. What if they overcame their shyness with her and earned her favor? Even though they might have hated her for what her people had done to theirs, he'd also wondered at the time if they had been interested in the bonny lass instead. It seemed that was the case. Maybe they even thought she had turned them because she was smitten with them!

There was one other way to rectify the situation. She would sit at the head table with him, his brothers, and his sister. Then Mege and the other lasses, who might show some interest in Alasdair, would see it was a lost cause. And so would Cleary and Baine if they had an interest in Isobel.

7

That afternoon, the dynamics had changed again between Isobel and Alasdair. To her surprise, Hans pulled her away from speaking to Elene and Bessetta before they sat down in the great hall to eat and told Isobel she was sitting next to Alasdair at the head table.

Bessetta smiled brightly. "It's about time my brother came to his senses."

Elene smiled just as cheerfully. "Enjoy your meal and everything else."

Isobel swore her face was bright red with embarrassment. But then she wondered if Alasdair had not been pleased that she had spoken to Cleary and Baine at the meal this morn. Or mayhap it was because of the interest the two brothers had shown in her.

She and Bessetta walked to the head table and then Isobel sat down next to Alasdair. "Did you want me to sit by you so you can keep me out of mischief?" She smiled at him, hoping the lasses who desired a mating with the wolf would believe they had no chance. Though she didn't believe she had made enough of an impression on him that he would want to mate her *either*. But she wasn't above playing the game.

"Aye."

"You know some of the women who are interested in vying for your attention will be envious that I'm sitting beside you and that they dinna have the pleasure."

He laughed. "If I had been interested in any of them in return, they would be sitting here with me instead."

His words surprised her. She really had thought he was trying to keep her from causing any further trouble with the newly turned wolves.

"Lorne says you're doing a great job guarding the keep."

"It's easy. No one is sneaking toward the castle to fight you." She was glad for that.

"Most likely if anyone tried it, they'll come at dark. Though we never leave anything to chance. If we didn't post guards during the day, that's when we'd have an attack for sure. But we also have wolf patrols at night. For us, we can still see what's going on at night when my enemies are at a disadvantage and our wolves can keep a lower profile."

"I agree. Lorne didn't mention to me that he would put me on that duty." She figured he just hadn't gotten around to it. Maybe he scheduled guards to do it for a longer period of time so they wouldn't have sleep issues as much with switching back and forth from day to night duty.

"He asked me if I wanted to have you serve as a wolf on guard duty at night, but I said no. I want you to be at the croft at night and you and Conall can keep your family and the crofters safe, should you encounter trouble."

"Thank you." She appreciated that Alasdair would want her to keep her family safe at night. It was probably true that should they have trouble, the enemy would arrive when everyone was sleeping. She was glad his telling Lorne not to put her on wolf guard duty wasn't because he wanted her watched while she pulled guard duty, or because he thought she couldn't fight as well as his Scottish warriors.

But his comment that she would continue to stay with the crofters meant he wasn't interested in taking her as a mate or she'd be staying at the keep instead. She felt a modicum of disappointment because of that.

"How many enemies *do* you have?" The clan her family had joined had been powerful, so they didn't fight with other clans very often.

"Too many to count. Does that make you want to leave and find someplace that is less—dangerous?" He drank from his tankard of ale.

She laughed. "I'm sure we ended up in the best place we could have since you are wolves also. And we will be eager to help your cause, but also most of your pack seem to have no animosity for us, which is always a concern."

"Other than the lassies who are glaring daggers at you."

She smiled. *That* she could deal with. "Why do you have so many enemies?"

"Others want what we have. 'Tis easier to steal from others than to put in the hard work to build it yourself."

"The castle." Land, power. She understood that.

"Aye. We have allied with clans who are enemies to others, and so we have made enemies of those. But you canna survive without making alliances. Because of what we have and how prosperous we are, I have had several offers to wed lasses."

Isobel raised a brow as she lifted her tankard of mead to her lips. "None suited? Or are you still pondering a new alliance or an old one?" She was disappointed with the notion that he might end up with someone else that he already had his sights set on.

"They are no' wolves, so I'm no' interested. The woman I will mate will have to be a royal wolf. One who can have my royal bairns. I have no intention of turning a woman, nor of dealing with the fallout with her family when she canna see them when she wants, or they wish to see her, and she is having trouble with her shifting. Nor do I want to have offspring who are not from royal lines. Life would be so much harder for them because they would have shifting difficulties also as they grew up."

"Aye. I agree. I had talked to the bairns about never shifting in front of humans, ever. And when they were running as wolves with either Conall or me, they were never to show themselves to humans. If they ever came across one, they were never to bite him or her."

"Sage advice. We tell our young ones the same."

"But we are all royals so we can shift at will. I have told you my story—how my father, mother, uncle, and aunt died, and how we were living among people who were not of our clan. What about you? How did you become clan chief? Did your da rule the clan before that?"

"My parents died young in a skirmish with other clans. My uncle, my da's brother, never had a mate or offspring. He was in charge of a pack of ten. During a battle with another clan, he was killed. I was older and for some time had been helping him to run the pack as if I was his son. I immediately ended up taking over the pack and expanding it as soon as I could. We needed more wolf numbers, but we had to ensure they were wolves that would go along with my rule, or we would have just had infighting and chaos."

"Like when I decided to bite Cleary and Baine without your approval."

Alasdair smiled at her. "You remind me of me—in a good way. Sometimes impetuous, but fair minded and protective of kin."

They talked about the plans he had for his people, growing

their wolf numbers, finishing the wall, adding the portcullis, and expanding the castle. She wanted to be part of all of it. She swore the meal lasted much longer than it normally did, and she figured she was the reason for it, though no one seemed to be eager to get back to work so it might have been a good thing. Except that the women who didn't like her already were still eyeing her with animosity.

When they finished eating the meal, Alasdair and Isobel walked outside of the keep together, both bound to do their duty. But she felt lighthearted, eager to see him tonight at the loch. She couldn't wait.

After the meal, he had to speak with his brothers about business while Isobel went up to the wall walk to pull her guard duty.

To her surprise, the dark-haired Mege came up the stairs to see her. "You are naught but a wild Viking—dangerous to our own people. Dinna think your kind will mate our pack leader."

"If 'tis something we both feel the need to do, we'll do it." Isobel had no intention of pretending it might not happen.

"Accidents do happen out here."

Isobel raised a brow. "And you think if I should 'accidentally' suffer an accident, his lairdship wouldna realize someone had done it on purpose to injure or kill me to keep me from mating him?"

Mege shrugged. "People are being injured or killed all the time. Just so you know."

"Thank you for the warning. I canna imagine you are the one who would actually do the deed though. Would you put one of your kin up to it? It would be a shame should that happen, if he gets caught at it and is punished for the misdeed instead of the one who came up with the idea. Though he would still be punished for committing the wrong."

"You think you're so clever."

"Aye. I am. When you have to work as hard as I did to stay alive and to ensure my kin did also, you have to be prepared for anything." Isobel had been so glad that Alasdair had taken her and her kin into his pack. Everyone seemed to like them, showing no animosity for them being Icelanders, but now this? She couldn't believe she'd stirred up so much attention among some of the eligible maids because the laird had showed some interest in her.

Mege finally said, "You willna sit at the head table with him this eve."

As if Mege could decide such a thing! "Why is that? If Alasdair wishes me to, I will. If he doesna, then I willna. So mayhap you are right. We will know for sure this very eve, will we no'?"

Mege scoffed and then turned on her heel and hurried off down the stairs to the inner bailey and headed inside the keep.

Isobel always watched her back so if someone was out to get her, she would be guarding for trouble, as long as no one put her own kin in danger because of her.

Then she began watching for any sign of anyone approaching the castle, but she suspected nothing would happen out there. Not until night, if anything was to happen. Now she was more concerned about herself with regard to Mege and her family or her friends though.

Once she was relieved of her duty, she headed downstairs to see if she was sitting with Elene to have the evening meal, or with Alasdair, which would irritate Mege even more. Mege caught her eye and was glaring at her as if she thought Isobel would heed her words and tell Alasdair she wouldn't sit with him if he asked her to.

Alasdair smiled at her, wordlessly telling Isobel where he wanted her to sit. Bessetta actually came to her table and said, "My brother wants you to join him at the head table."

Hans spoke to Alasdair and then he came to speak with her.

Isobel was surprised both his sister and his brother would speak with her. Maybe Hans wasn't going to tell her to sit with Alasdair. When Hans joined her, he said, "Unless Alasdair says otherwise, he wants you to sit with him at the head table."

"I told you so," Bessetta said.

"I'm glad to." Isobel smiled at Elene and then went with Hans and Bessetta to the head table, dying to give Mege a look that said she was sitting with the laird, so what was *she* going to do about it? But Isobel figured the woman was angry enough already and instead pretended she didn't care how Mege viewed this.

When Isobel sat next to Alasdair, he said, "I'm glad you decided to join me."

"I couldna presume you wanted me to sit beside you for further meals."

"Well, I do. Rory said Mege went to talk to you on the wall walk earlier today when you were pulling your guard duty."

"She did."

"No one can get away with much without someone noticing something."

"You are having me guarded?" she asked, surprised, but pleased that he would think of her safety like that, if he had.

Alasdair smiled. "My brothers are watching out for you, it seems. They said that they've heard from several that Mege has been spreading rumors about you being dangerous to the pack. So Rory wanted to make sure she wasn't threatening you."

"She was, but I can take care of myself." Even though Isobel felt that way, she wasn't going to pretend Mege hadn't threatened her, because if she followed through with it, someone in the clan was going to die for it. Maybe Isobel, or the person who came after her. She was sure Mege wouldn't have the courage or the ability to try and kill Isobel herself. Though Mege would be the instigator and she and her kin would be banished if any harm came to Isobel, she figured.

"No one threatens anyone who is under my protection."

"It doesna mean she will carry through with her threat—"

"That was?"

"I could meet with an accident."

Alasdair cast a stern look in Mege's direction. She had been watching Alasdair and Isobel but quickly looked at her meal.

"I dinna want to involve your kin in this. I will be careful to watch my back," Isobel said, though she did worry about her own kin should Mege or her family or friends take the interest the laird was showing to Isobel out on her family.

"Aye, you will. But I canna have you harmed by someone in my clan either. I will be discussing this with Mege and her family to set them straight if anyone thinks to do anything."

"Thank you." Isobel was glad he didn't act as though it wasn't important, just in case Mege followed through with her threat.

"So tonight, I'll be at the loch." He raised a brow to wait for her response.

She smiled. "I'll be there to guard you."

But the expression on his face said he didn't want her to be there so that she could guard him. If Mege knew where they would both be tonight, she'd probably want to kill them herself!

8

A lasdair was glad his brothers were watching out for Isobel. He would be too, but whoever wished her harm was keeping it quiet around him. That Mege would even threaten Isobel like that, whether it was a case of just bluffing or not, was enough to make him want to banish her from the pack. He was a fair leader, he felt, but when it came to the safety of his people, all his pack members, he took something like that seriously.

After the meal, he called a meeting with Mege and her father, mother, and three brothers. He didn't want them to leave the pack. But he had to make it clear that whoever he chose for a mate, it would be his decision, and no one would stop that from happening. And if they couldn't live with it, they were free to leave the pack now.

"Word spreads throughout a pack so quickly, I'm sure you have some idea why I've come here to speak with you," Alasdair said.

"Whatever the Viking woman has told you, she lies," Mege quickly said, as if he would believe her word over Isobel's.

"If you wish to leave the pack, you are welcome to. If any

harm comes to Isobel or her kin, I will hold you and your kin responsible for it," Alasdair told Mege's da. Mayhap he could control his own daughter. In any event, Alasdair wanted them to know that he wouldn't allow any harm to come to Isobel or the others.

"What was said to start this dialogue?" Mege's da asked, sounding puzzled.

"Ask Mege. She has threatened Isobel, stating an accident could befall her if she pursues seeing me further as a prospective mate. 'Tis my decision, no' anyone else's," Alasdair said.

Her da agreed. "Aye, as it should be." He gave Mege a dark look.

Alasdair assumed he'd speak with her and set her straight. But when he considered her brothers' expressions, he knew she had approached them about wanting Isobel harmed. They looked guilty enough and he smelled their worried scent. Not only that, but they glanced from him to their da as if they knew he'd give them the devil over it next.

Their da eyed them with concern.

"We dinna want to leave the pack," Mege's mother said. "My daughter knows her place. If there is any trouble between her and anyone else you might consider as your mate, we will deal with her." She cast a dark look at her sons. "None of us will stand in your way. We welcome the north wolves to the pack. They will help us to fight our enemies. They bring new blood to the pack. It is good."

"Aye," Mege's da said. "The family of the northern region has endured hardships we have no' had to face once we joined your pack. We willna leave unless you wish it. I, and my kin, will protect them with our lives, just as we pledge the same to you and your kin and the rest of the pack."

Alasdair inclined his head to the mother and father. Alasdair looked at the brothers. They inclined their heads to him, telling him they would do as he asked. Then Alasdair stood and everyone in the family rose to their feet.

"I dinna believe I need to say anything further to you about this," Alasdair said.

"Nay, you should never have had to speak to us about this in the first place," the da said. "We will take care of matters here."

Alasdair nodded, but he didn't bother to look at Mege. She was lucky she was still part of the pack. She showed no sign of remorse and she had lied to make Isobel appear to be the guilty party. At least her parents could tell she was lying, and they would have words with their sons also. He would not have that kind of behavior in his pack. They needed to be united as a pack.

Despite the family's assurances, he felt troubled that it had come to this in the first place, all because of a woman's spitefulness.

But then he thought of seeing Isobel at the loch and he smiled. She made the world right for him all over again.

He stalked out of the keep and Hans intercepted him. "Is everything all right?" Hans asked.

"Aye. It is now."

Hans smiled. "You havena had trouble like this for some time, not within the pack. Sometimes you need to have a wee bit to awaken the senses."

Alasdair chuckled. "Aye."

"Are you going to the loch, perchance?"

"Aye."

"Do you need anyone to guard your back?" Hans asked, still sounding like he worried about him.

"Nay. We have this covered."

"Isobel and you."

"And her nephew, if we should need him."

"Aye, and Dawy and Agnes are good fighters. But if you need our help, howl, and we will come to your aid."

"Thanks, brother."

When Alasdair went to the loch to swim, he hoped Isobel would come out of the croft to join him. But when he finally arrived there, he smelled Isobel's wild wolf scent. He took a deep breath and hurried through the Rowan bushes to join her if she was there and hadn't just been in the area recently.

When he actually saw her naked by the loch, getting ready to enter the water, his heart skipped a beat. No other lass had ever made him feel so drawn to her.

Her freed blond hair was whipping about her shoulders and breasts in the warm breeze. Creamy white skin, rosy nipples, curly blond hair between her thighs covering her more intimate parts were all revealed as she waded into the loch. Aye, he had it bad for her.

But he wasn't planning on guarding her from the shore. He stepped out of the rowan shrubs to show her he was there, not intending to sneak up on her. She had already entered the water and was swimming.

He called out to her, "Did you want me to join you, or do you want me to guard you?"

She whipped around and gave him the most beautiful smile. "If you're not afraid of me, you can join me in the loch."

"I can protect you in the water."

She laughed.

Then he stripped off his clothes, and he swore that whenever he did it to bathe or swim or shift, it was just second nature, but with her watching him so studiously, he felt like he was getting ready to mate her. And his body was reacting in a way that said he was way too interested in her.

She was smiling like she was amused she had aroused him

so. Then he walked into the loch, dove in, and swam out to see her.

"I was hoping you would join me out here. I hadna thought you would be here already," he said.

"I planned to swim before you got here so I could guard you properly. But then here you are. Joining me instead."

He pulled her into his arms and kissed her. "I am going to have to mate you."

"Is that so?" Isobel asked, holding him close.

"Aye, it's the only way I can truly protect you—"

"And I can protect you?" She raised her brows.

"Aye, exactly." He kissed her deeply and she kissed him back with the same kind of passion. "I have spoken to Mege and her family. You will have no more trouble from her. It doesna change the way I feel about you."

"You dinna think it is too soon? For us to mate each other? Dinna you think we should wait until your people are more accepting of us?"

"Nay. I have waited for you all my life. I have dreamed of you."

"Nay." She sounded like she couldn't believe him.

"Aye. We were meant to be together. When you had first arrived, I hadna known if you had come with a force of Vikings to invade our land. But I knew I wanted you from that first moment I saw you. How do you feel about it?"

"I was much impressed with you also. *Ja*, you are mine."

He smiled and loved her. "You will be my mate and rule my pack jointly with me."

"I love you. I would never have thought saving my family would come to this, finding a wolf mate, who happened to be a pack leader in Scotia, finding a home for them that would be safe for them."

"Making my dreams come true. I love you."

They kissed again, but he was trying to figure out where to take her so that they could consummate their love for one another in a mating. He didn't want to take her all the way back to the keep. Not this minute.

She smiled at him. "The bracken will do."

"Are you sure?"

"Aye. What were you thinking? We canna do it in the crofter's hut. Not with everyone in there. And walking to the keep will take too long."

"That's what I was thinking. Then in the bracken it is."

They swam to the shore and he grabbed up their brats and carried them through the bracken. Once they found the perfect spot, they laid the brats down on the ground, spreading them out, creating a makeshift bed surrounded by green ferns that stretched toward the sky, the full moon illuminating the dark sky, loch, and the tops of the bracken.

It seemed the perfect place to mate his wild Viking wolf. He laid her down on the brats and began kissing her soft mouth meant for *just* kissing him. She ran her hand through his wet hair, and he loved the intimacy between them. No woman had ever done that to him before. She kissed his mouth back, her kisses just as rampant, desirous, filling him with an unquenchable need.

Her heart was beating the same rhythm as his, hard and fast as he moved his head down her body, trailing kisses from her mouth to her breast. He licked and suckled on the rigid nipple and then began to work on the other, giving it its due.

She moaned, her eyes shut as she took deep breaths every time he licked a nipple, and then he kissed the one and suckled and released.

"Join me," she whispered, as if she couldn't wait to be mated to him. Maybe she was afraid someone would come looking for him and she didn't want to be caught in the middle of the act. He didn't believe she'd think he'd change his mind if he didn't hurry.

But he wasn't about to rush through the first mating between them. He slid his hand down her smooth belly and found her blond curly hairs. He nudged his fingers through them until he located her woman's bud, swollen, aroused. His staff was as stiff as a pike already, and he truly wanted to mate her as quickly as possible, yet he had to show her how important it was to him to pleasure her also.

"I'm ready," she said softly, before he began to stroke her nubbin.

Yeah, she was, but not like he suspected she thought. When he began stroking her, she moaned. "Oh, goddess, what—are—" She bit her lip, unable to speak further and he kissed her mouth while he continued to run his finger over her nub.

She was wet for him, ready for his staff, and moving her hips to get even more pleasure from his touch. Her heart was beating even more wildly now, and he tongued her mouth while she sucked on his tongue with desperation, trying to reach the climax, but he suspected no one had ever pleasured her in this way.

She nipped at his lip, and he smiled, but then her face tensed, and she gritted her teeth, growling, embracing the wolf and woman as she cried out with joy.

He immediately hoped no one would hear her and think she was in peril and come to the rescue. He kissed her mouth then, licking her lips, nipping on her lower one. "Are you ready?"

"For you to be mine and only mine," she said softly. "*Ja*, aye, I am."

He wanted to ask if she'd ever been with a man like this, not wanting to hurt her for the first time, but he couldn't ask without it sounding like he wouldn't like it if she had been. So he treated her as though she was a virgin, slowly pushing into her, as much as he wanted to begin thrusting, he was so ready.

He went cautiously until he felt a barrier. She was so tight, he was certain she'd never been with anyone before like this.

She held her breath and then released and breathed through the pain. And then he pushed all the way in and began to thrust. Not hard, but enough to keep the momentum going.

Her inner core was still gripping him in waves of climax and then he released in a burst and growled out, "Isobel, gods you are mine."

She smiled at him as he kissed her again. "Hmm, and you are mine."

As wolves, she could have made love all the way with a human, and not been mated. With wolves, it would have been a mating and they couldn't be with another wolf, unless they lost their mate. Oftentimes, a wolf who lost his mate wouldn't take another. But she hadn't been with another man, and he was glad he was her first.

"Was it good—" he started to say, and she pushed him off her and straddled him, then kissed him deeply.

"Oh, aye. I never knew a man could pleasure a woman like that."

"Aww, lass, you deserve to be pleasured like that every time and more." He ran his hand over her thighs.

And then she snuggled up against him, her head on his chest. "As much as I don't want to ever leave our little fortress of ferns, someone's going to be missing you."

"And you. But aye, we need to get dressed." Not only because he worried his brothers would check up on him again—just to make sure he was safe, but also because he wanted to take her to the keep with him, to tell the rest of the pack that they were now mated wolves. That she was also now their pack leader.

9

Isobel loved being with Alasdair like this, hidden in the bracken, glad that they had mated, but she wondered what to do about her kin and the crofters as far as sleeping arrangements went. She didn't want to take the young ones to live with her in the castle when the crofters wanted a family so bad, and her nephews and niece seemed to adore Agnes and Dawy. Isobel had to admit they treated them like their own bairns, only not as distantly or harshly as their own da had done, which all had to do with the hard life they had been faced with after their mother had died. Conall was such a help to the crofters too and he seemed eager to learn shepherding and growing crops also.

"What do we do about the living arrangements?" she asked Alasdair, running her hand over his bare chest, her cheek resting against it.

"I've considered the situation and I believe we should let it be up to your nephews and niece. Agnes and Dawy will abide by any decision they make. Of course they would like to keep the rest of your family at the croft, but it's ultimately your kin's decision. You know I will want you at the castle from now on."

"Guarding it."

"Guarding me." He kissed her. "As I will guard you. The crofters have never had any trouble before. If they ever believe they will, they will turn into their wolves and escape to the castle. I have watched Conall fighting with the others in practice combat when he is not building the wall. He is a formidable opponent, despite his youth. Even young Drummond is quite handy with the sword. Both of them will help Dawy if he ever has difficulties with encroaching neighbors."

"Aye. We teach all bairn how to fight. Even Libby will be fighting like I did."

Alasdair nodded. She was glad he didn't see anything wrong in the women fighting. She would teach his women to fight also, if he wished it.

"And this eve?" she asked.

"'Tis late. I need to be getting back to the keep before my brothers send a rescue force. I wish to take you with me though."

She wanted to go with Alasdair in the worst way tonight, but she felt she had to discuss this matter with Conall and the bairns before she just abandoned them. And she didn't want to wake the wee ones or disturb the crofters' sleep this eve as late as it was.

"I will stay the night at the croft and discuss this in the morn with my kin and Dawy and Agnes and see what everyone wants to do. But on the morrow, I'll stay with you no matter what my kin agrees to do as far as living arrangements go."

"All right. I understand." He kissed her again and then he said, "Wait here. I'll gather our clothes."

She waited for a few minutes, listening to Alasdair as he moved through the bracken, but then she heard a startled gasp and a thud. She shifted into her wolf and ran through the bracken, hoping she would find nothing the matter, but afraid she would locate her mate sprawled out on the ground. Which was just what she discovered. Three men were headed for the croft, their backs to her, and Alasdair was lying on the beach where she and he had left the rest of their clothes.

She was so angry, she could have killed every last one of the men. But she had to warn her family and the crofters of danger and then see to Alasdair. She dashed back into the bracken and howled to wake Dawy and Agnes and her family. And she howled to warn Alasdair's pack that they were in danger.

To her surprise, the men who were headed toward the house stopped, and all three of them turned to peer at the bracken before she came out to help Alasdair and protect him. One of the men called out, "Inge?"

She peered out of the bracken, recognizing the deep voice, though it was much deeper than what she had remembered. That's when she recognized a scent drifting on the breeze too —it was her twin brother's scent, but he'd been lost at sea. Only her family and Elene knew her name was Inge from Iceland.

"It is me, Leif," he called out.

She left the bracken but heard wolves howl in the distance.

"What are you doing here?" Leif asked. "I thought you were a slave of these people."

She couldn't believe she was seeing her twin brother. During a violent storm while she and her parents and brother were sailing, he had been washed overboard and they'd never found him. He...he was alive. She stared at the man he had become, blond, tall, muscular, the other men darker haired, just as tall and muscular, Scotsmen, she thought.

"Who is she?" one of the men asked.

"My sister."

The door to the croft was thrown open and Dawy and Conall charged forth with swords in hand ready to kill their foe.

She shifted and threw on her chemise. "He is my brother,

your uncle, Conall." Then she saw to Alasdair. His forehead was bloodied, but he was coming to. "Alasdair is my mate."

They heard horses off in the distance and she knew her brother and these men would be killed for harming Alasdair. "What are you doing here?" Isobel asked, glad to see her brother, but she needed to know what their intent was.

"We smelled lots of wolves in the area and thought it was a pack and we might join them. But then I smelled your scent here and thought these people had taken you hostage," Leif said. "I came to free you."

She wasn't sure they'd let them join the pack now. "Help me with Alasdair."

Leif came over to help Alasdair sit up, and then her mate looked at her, his eyes not focusing at first. Then he saw Leif and reached for his sword.

"He is my brother, come to rescue me," she quickly said.

"The one lost at sea?" Alasdair asked, frowning.

"Aye, but he has found me." She looked at the other men. "I dinna know the other men, but they are wolves also." She and her brother helped Alasdair into his tunic, and then she went to get their brats so they could finish dressing before Alasdair's forces arrived.

"I grew up with them," Leif said about the men with him, staying with Alasdair to assist him while she returned with their brats.

"The three of you are on your own?" Isobel asked.

"Aye," Leif said. "The brothers lost their parents to a sickness after they had taken me in and so the three of us have been working where we can and living off the land. They took me in because I'm a wolf also, taught me the language, clothed me and fed me until their parents died and then we were on our own."

The horses were growing closer, and Isobel howled as a human to tell the ones coming to rescue them that everything was all right so that the pack members wouldn't try and kill her brother and the other men.

"Did I hear right? That you mated the pack leader?" Conall asked.

"Aye. I just didna think my long-lost brother would show up and nearly kill him."

"I am sorry," Leif said to both her and to Alasdair. "He is the pack leader?" He carefully helped Alasdair to stand.

"Aye, I am. And so is Isobel now too," Alasdair said, unsteady on his feet.

"Do you want to go inside the croft?" Conall asked.

"Aye," Dawy said. "Bring him inside."

"You will join my pack," Alasdair said to Leif, showing no ill will toward him and his friends. "We have need of able-bodied men such as yourself. You can help build the wall, live in the barracks, and eat with us."

She was proud of Alasdair and glad she had mated him. He could have handled this situation so much differently. She knew her former chieftain would have. For striking him? His warriors would have killed Leif.

The horses were nearly upon them. Hans and Rory were leading ten men to the croft and soon surrounded them before Leif and Conall could assist Alasdair to the croft.

"What has happened here?" Hans asked, dismounting, and helping Alasdair as Isobel was gathering up Alasdair's and her weapons.

"Everything is secure," Alasdair said, though his forehead was bloodied, and he was still wavering a bit where he stood.

"Aye and who hit you?" Hans asked, none of the other men dismounting.

"I did. I thought my sister had been taken as a slave. The last thing I knew about her whereabouts was she was in Iceland.

Now she's here? What was I to think when I smelled Inge's scent here?"

"That I had made a home here like you have done. This is Alasdair's brother Hans, and the other is Rory. This is my brother Leif," Isobel said. "And I go by Isobel now, Leif."

"And we are mated," Alasdair said as Leif and Hans took him inside the croft. He sat down on a chair at the table and Agnes quickly washed the blood off his head and bandaged it with a spare cloth.

Libby and Drummond were looking on, wide-eyed, though Drummond was holding his small sword, in preparation for a fight.

Isobel explained to Leif who Conall was.

"Boldof?" Leif said in surprise. "You were a wee bairn when I saw you last." And then he met the younger siblings. They hadn't been born before Leif was lost at sea. "My niece and nephews." He gave everyone bear hugs, sounding delighted to have found some of his family again, but when she told him all their parents had died, he was saddened to hear it.

"What do you want us to do with them?" Hans asked Alasdair.

"I'm going with Alasdair to the keep," Isobel said, deciding the matter for them. "My brother will stay with his niece and nephews to provide security and to get to know them." She knew the crofters would be pleased the bairns were staying with them. "If that is all right with you and Agnes," she said to them. "And if it is all right with you, Conall, Drummond, Libby."

"Aye," Conall said, and everyone agreed with him.

"In the morn, we can break our fast together," Isobel said. "And Leif's friends can come with us and stay in the barracks."

Alasdair smiled at her. "We do as the lass says. She is now your pack leader also."

For wolf pack leaders, it was different than if Alasdair had just been a clan leader in which the wife might not have a lot of say in the leadership of the clan. Isobel would help rule the pack just like her husband. And he seemed to appreciate how she'd handled the situation when he appeared a little out of it for now.

Hans helped Alasdair onto his horse and then lifted Isobel behind him to make sure her mate didn't fall from Hans's mount. Hans joined Rory on his horse, and two other riders gave both brothers a lift. They said good night to the crofters and Isobel's family and rode back to the keep.

"I think you did this on purpose," Isobel said, hugging Alasdair tightly. Not because she thought he might fall off the horse, but because she loved feeling his hard body pressed tightly against her.

"Encouraged your brother to hit me?" Alasdair sounded like he wasn't following her line of reasoning.

"Aye. So that I'd come home with you tonight and he would stay with the rest of my family, and all would be well."

Alasdair grunted. "He hit me hard."

"Aye, but he didna kill you."

"Which is why I'm taking the lot of them into the pack."

"Because they can help build your wall."

"Our wall." He turned his head to look at her, and she kissed him on the cheek.

She sighed. "I love you. Thank you for taking them in, despite what my brother had done to you."

"I love you, Isobel. You saved me when I couldn't save myself. Your quick action both in warning the crofters and the pack proved to me just how invaluable you are. And then telling them that all was well before unnecessary blood was shed? You will make a great pack leader."

"As fair minded as you, I should hope."

"Aye. You will be. It is the reason I continue to rule the pack."

They finally arrived at the keep, and Hans said, "We willna

wake you in the morn, but bring food to you in your chamber when you wish to break your fast."

"And a celebration is in order also," Rory said.

Alasdair smiled. "Aye."

"When he is feeling better," Isobel said.

The brothers smiled at Alasdair. "It seems you have met your match."

Alasdair chuckled. "Aye, she is perfect for me."

Then he and Isobel retired to his own chamber, and she helped him to undress. She thought he was just going to climb into bed, but he wanted to help her disarm first, and pull off her shoes, brat, léine, and chemise, then join him in bed.

"Are you truly feeling all right?" she asked, snuggling with him under the furs, worried about him.

"Aye. I canna believe my fortune when your brother came along so I could take you home with me."

She sighed and kissed his chest. "I'm sorry he hit you. But you have to admit you are adding more able-bodied wolves to the pack."

He chuckled and kissed the top of her head, his hand sliding down her back in a gentle caress. "You do realize that you have added eight wolves to the pack since your arrival? I have you to thank for that."

And, she was thinking, she would add even more to the pack with her loving mate in time.

EPILOGUE

Not only was there feasting galore for two weeks straight once the pack learned that Isobel and Alasdair had mated, they had wed each other too. The wall and portcullis were finally finished with the additional help of their new pack members.

Mege wasn't happy that Alasdair had mated Isobel so she had tried to show interest in the next wolf who was in command after Alasdair and Isobel, should anything happen to them. But Hans wasn't interested in her, especially since she'd wanted to mate Alasdair first and had threatened Isobel with harm should she have continued to pursue the pack leader. Mege was lucky she was still with the pack. Mege had been saying all along that Isobel would never provide bairns to the clan. Four months later, Isobel proved her wrong.

Only one clan had tried to cause problems for them since Isobel and her family and Elene had arrived, but with Alasdair and Isobel's extended wolf pack, Isobel's constant work with the women to prepare them to be part of the fighting force, and the castle fortifications, they had done well against the incursion and their enemies had been vanquished.

The clan had even brought Isobel's uncle's longboat hidden in the cave to the loch and refitted it to look like one of their own. Alasdair had fastened the dragon masthead to the wall in their bedchamber to honor the symbol of the strength and bravery of Isobel and her kin and their friend's journey. The bairns learned to row, to sail, and to fish from it. Isobel's brother and the rest of her kin continued to stay with the crofters which delighted them and also they were better protected now that her brother was with them.

As wolves that night, Isobel and Alasdair ran to the cliffs to see the ocean in all its glory where she had first come ashore and found a new world that had awaited her. The moon in the dark sky shone across the choppy ocean, a storm off in the distance coming in, fog covering the beach. She howled with joy to be here with Alasdair, the beautiful wolf and man combined who had taken her, her kin, and their Highland friend in. And now she was carrying Alasdair's bairns, unsure just how many— but as wolves, there was no telling. She couldn't be gladder to be here with him, his family, and the rest of the pack.

∽

ALASDAIR HOWLED AS WELL, telling the world he was with the she-wolf of his dreams and licked Isobel's face. She licked his back. He adored her and couldn't be happier that he had found her and brought her home, that she was having their bairns, and that they finally had a home that was safe from invasion. He loved her family as much as she loved his and he was glad how this had all worked out. He'd always wondered if the clan she'd been with would ever come looking for her and her family, but he felt assured they wouldn't bother and wouldn't even know where Isobel and the others had ended up. They probably wouldn't believe that Isobel and the others had survived the trip, if they even had considered they might come here. But if the clan Isobel and her family had been with ever did show up here, their wolf pack would take care of them.

With the approaching storm growing closer, he and Isobel raced back to the keep, the guards quickly opening the portcullis for them. He loved that they'd finished the wall and the gates, and his people were all the more protected.

He and Isobel ran inside the castle through a special door they'd created for wolves, though the hunting hounds had learned to use it also. Alasdair and Isobel ran up the curved stairs to their own chamber for lots more loving. Other business could wait; *this* never could.

ACKNOWLEDGMENTS

Thanks so much to Darla Taylor, Donna Fournier, and Lor Melvin who are always up for beta reading something new! Lor returns after finally retiring from her job at the school and I couldn't be more thrilled! Hope you all enjoy the Medieval Highland wolf novella, something I've always wanted to write!

ABOUT THE AUTHOR

Author Bio

USA Today bestselling and award-winning author **Terry Spear** has written over a hundred paranormal romance novels, young adult, and medieval Highland historical romances. Her first werewolf romance, *Heart of the Wolf,* was named a 2008 *Publishers Weekly*'s Best Book of the Year, and her subsequent titles have garnered high praise and hit the *USA Today* bestseller list. A retired officer of the U.S. Army Reserves, Terry lives in Spring, Texas, where she is working on her next werewolf romance, shapeshifting jaguars, cougar shifters, vampires, hot Highlanders, and having fun with her young adult novels, helping with her granddaughter and grandson and raising two Havanese.

For more information, please visit her website at: http://www.terryspear.com

Blog:

Follow her for new releases and book deals: www.bookbub.com/authors/terry-spear

Twitter: @TerrySpear.

Facebook: http://www.facebook.com/terry.spear

ALSO BY TERRY SPEAR

Heart of the Cougar Series:

Cougar's Mate, Book 1

Call of the Cougar, Book 2

Taming the Wild Cougar, Book 3

Covert Cougar Christmas (Novella)

Double Cougar Trouble, Book 4

Cougar Undercover, Book 5

Cougar Magic, Book 6

Cougar Halloween Mischief (Novella)

Falling for the Cougar, Book 7

Catch the Cougar (A Halloween Novella)

Cougar Christmas Calamity Book 8

You Had Me at Cougar, Book 9

Saving the White Cougar, Book 10

∾

Heart of the Bear Series

Loving the White Bear, Book 1

Claiming the White Bear, Book 2

∾

The Highlanders Series:

Novella Prequels:

His Wild Highland #1, Vexing the Highlander #2

Winning the Highlander's Heart, The Accidental Highland Hero, Highland Rake, Taming the Wild Highlander, The Highlander, Her Highland Hero, The Viking's Highland Lass, My Highlander

Other historical romances: Lady Caroline & the Egotistical Earl, A Ghost of a Chance at Love

∽

Heart of the Wolf Series: Heart of the Wolf, Destiny of the Wolf, To Tempt the Wolf, Legend of the White Wolf, Seduced by the Wolf, Wolf Fever, Heart of the Highland Wolf, Dreaming of the Wolf, A SEAL in Wolf's Clothing, A Howl for a Highlander, A Highland Werewolf Wedding, A SEAL Wolf Christmas, Silence of the Wolf, Hero of a Highland Wolf, A Highland Wolf Christmas, A SEAL Wolf Hunting; A Silver Wolf Christmas, A SEAL Wolf in Too Deep, Alpha Wolf Need Not Apply, Billionaire in Wolf's Clothing, Between a Rock and a Hard Place, SEAL Wolf Undercover, Dreaming of a White Wolf Christmas, Flight of the White Wolf, All's Fair in Love and Wolf, A Billionaire Wolf for Christmas, SEAL Wolf Surrender (2019), Silver Town Wolf: Home for the Holidays (2019), Wolff Brothers: You Had Me at Wolf, Night of the Billionaire Wolf, Joy to the Wolves (Red Wolf), The Wolf Wore Plaid, Jingle Bell Wolf, Best of Both Wolves, While the Wolf's Away, Christmas Wolf Surprise, Wolf Takes the Lead, Wolf on the Wild Side

SEAL Wolves: To Tempt the Wolf, A SEAL in Wolf's Clothing, A SEAL Wolf Christmas, A SEAL Wolf Hunting, A SEAL Wolf in Too Deep, SEAL Wolf Undercover, SEAL Wolf Surrender (2019)

Silver Bros Wolves: Destiny of the Wolf, Wolf Fever, Dreaming of the Wolf, Silence of the Wolf, A Silver Wolf Christmas, Alpha Wolf Need Not Apply, Between a Rock and a Hard Place, All's Fair in Love and Wolf, Silver Town Wolf: Home for the Holidays

Wolff Brothers of Silver Town Wolff Brothers: You Had Me at Wolf

Arctic Wolves: Legend of the White Wolf, Dreaming of a White Wolf Christmas, Flight of the White Wolf, While the Wolf's Away

Billionaire Wolves: Billionaire in Wolf's Clothing, A Billionaire Wolf for Christmas, Night of the Billionaire Wolf

Highland Wolves: Heart of the Highland Wolf, A Howl for a Highlander, A Highland Werewolf Wedding, Hero of a Highland Wolf, A Highland Wolf Christmas, The Wolf Wore Plaid,

Red Wolf Series: Seduced by the Wolf, Joy to the Wolves, Best of Both Wolves,

Novellas: A United Shifter Force Christmas

Highland Wolves of Old: Wolf Pack (Book I)

Heart of the Jaguar Series: Savage Hunger, Jaguar Fever, Jaguar Hunt, Jaguar Pride, A Very Jaguar Christmas, You Had Me at Jaguar

Novella: The Witch and the Jaguar

Dawn of the Jaguar

Romantic Suspense: Deadly Fortunes, In the Dead of the Night, Relative Danger, Bound by Danger

Vampire romances: Killing the Bloodlust, Deadly Liaisons, Huntress for Hire, Forbidden Love, Vampire Redemption, Primal Desire

Vampire Novellas: Vampiric Calling, The Siren's Lure, Seducing the Huntress

Other Romance: Exchanging Grooms, Marriage, Las Vegas Style

~

Science Fiction Romance: Galaxy Warrior

Teen/Young Adult/Fantasy Books

The World of Fae:

The Dark Fae, Book 1

The Deadly Fae, Book 2

The Winged Fae, Book 3

The Ancient Fae, Book 4

Dragon Fae, Book 5

Hawk Fae, Book 6

Phantom Fae, Book 7

Golden Fae, Book 8

Falcon Fae, Book 9

Woodland Fae, Book 10

Angel Fae, Book 11

The World of Elf:

The Shadow Elf

Darkland Elf

Blood Moon Series:

Kiss of the Vampire

The Vampire...In My Dreams

Demon Guardian Series:

The Trouble with Demons

Demon Trouble, Too

Demon Hunter

Non-Series for Now:

Ghostly Liaisons

The Beast Within

Courtly Masquerade

Deidre's Secret

The Magic of Inherian:

The Scepter of Salvation

The Mage of Monrovia

Emerald Isle of Mists

Made in the USA
Las Vegas, NV
10 October 2023

78853026R00065